ALSO BY NICKLAUS SUINO

101 Ideas to Kick Your Ass Into Gear
(with Ian Gray)

Budo Mind and Body: Training Secrets of the Japanese
Martial Arts (comprehensive revision of Arts of Strength,
Arts of Serenity)

Arts of Strength, Arts of Serenity

Strategy in Japanese Swordsmanship

Practice Drills for Japanese Swordsmanship

The Art of Japanese Swordsmanship

The Drinking Game

The Drinking Game

Nicklaus Suino

Ann Arbor, Michigan

Master and Fool, LLC
3853 Research Park Drive, Suite 110
Ann Arbor, Michigan 48104

Copyright © 2013 Nicklaus Suino

Many of the activities described in this book are dangerous, unhealthy or deadly! Neither the authors or the publisher is responsible for the results of your choice to imitate the characters herein. You do so at your own risk.

10 9 8 7 6 5 4 3 2 1

FIRST EDITION

Written, Edited, and Printed in the United States of America

ISBN: 1481812912
ISBN-13: 978-1481812917

His body, bent forward from the hips, was perfectly straight, making his legs seem all the more unreliable. From below the thicket of dwarf bamboo, along the main road, came a sound of water down a narrow ditch. Nothing more – and yet the retreating figure of the Master somehow brought tears to my eyes. I was profoundly moved, for reasons I do not myself understand. In that figure walking absently from the game there was the still sadness of another world.

- from *The Master of Go* by Yasunari Kawabata

Dedicated to Mark Edward Suino,
for both the good and the bad.

Preamble

It may seem strange to write about honor in this day and age. It's difficult to convey the sense of responsibility Russell Aldridge felt about the ways of drinking he had practiced since the late nineteen thirties. We've become a nation of people who will sacrifice every dignity to win fame or a few dollars; not many of us have principles of any sort to defend. There may be no way to objectively measure who is right about how to do such and such a thing, but the old man felt his was the way drinking should be done and that other ways were for "women, fairies and damn fools."

So it was a bit more than a contest for him, I guess. Because, along with the erosion of sensible drinking habits, he had seen a long, slow slide in the the sensibilities of the average citizen toward the materialistic, childish, Twenty First Century American lifestyle. He supported a serious approach to certain activities in life, and among these were drinking, fishing and shooting pool.

None were to be corrupted by a lot of idle chatter. Just as it was self evident there was a best lure to throw in after a northern pike or a lake trout, it was clear to the old man that there were best subjects to discuss while drinking. These subjects included fishing and travel, and the way such stories were supposed to be told sweetened the passing time the way an occasional salted peanut improved the taste of beer. They were meant to be long and drawn out by pauses for beer and cigarettes. A diversion in the story line was acceptable if it illustrated some characteristic travel occurrence. Lies were essential. The way lies were worked into the story was a testament to the skill of the storyteller, and the weight of this measurement increased with the number of drinks consumed.

In their enthusiasm, younger men like his opponent, the industrial heating and cooling salesman Bob Santoni, were often caught up in the web of their own lies. An eight-pound brown trout was meant to stay an eight-pound brown trout during the course of the story and not mean to later emerge from the ice chest a fourteen-pound laker. The only way such a transformation could be justified was by a complex and at least partly plausible series of digressions and fantastic occurrences. Young men seldom had the patience to weave a properly tangled net, and never after more than a six pack. Neither all drinkers nor all storytellers were created equal.

Youth, or the disease of perpetual youthfulness, was the most common downfall in storytelling, or in life. Aldridge had seen too many kids race their boats out onto some lake he was fishing, scaring the fish, screaming and shouting, perhaps skiing over his favorite fishing hole, and only afterwards pulling up to him to ask, "how's the fishing?" The same sort race along the highways in their sedans or through the woods in their snowmobiles. Too often they're the ones who end up in jails, hospitals, or the morgue after being too anxious to get somewhere fast. Worse, they send others to the cemetery in their haste. I had heard the old man curse them many times for the loss of life and of the opportunity to pursue happiness, and that made me think my own social backwardness was one source of his fondness for me. He knew that I'd rather have spent a few hours quietly fishing on a lake than buzzing around it in a speedboat. Not only was it quieter, he would say, it was cheaper and more sensible.

We had plenty of talks about the right way to do things and I generally agreed with him, though I now think perhaps his was the healthier form of cynicism since it came with old age. He had seen Michigan change from a wilderness to a beehive of tourism and construction. It had been his birthplace, and he lived and traveled in the state nearly all his life. Most of the people he passed were tourists and trespassers. Nearly all knew far less than he about his passions, yet they had the more expensive boats, the flashier outdoor clothing, and there were far more of them.

In my own case, the passion for fishing, camping and talking over a beer was a way of retreating from the challenges of adult life. Instead of getting a job with a newspaper or teaching English, I kept driving a cab and taking week long vacations every few months. I told myself that fishing and traveling were more rewarding than living a regular life and working at a real job, but the truth is I hadn't really tried the latter. Relationships with people my own age were too difficult. Women were, at the time, as much a mystery as an attraction. Talking and drinking with the old man made all the day-to-day difficulties seem far away, and I could justify the time with him by imagining that the exposure to his wisdom was making me wise, too.

The truth about Mr. Aldridge's retrograde lifestyle is probably that he was the cause of his own failure to adjust to the changing times. All his activities could be considered simply ways to pass the time until death, if the enjoyment and dedication he brought to them were ignored. It's easier to sit inside a tavern and watch the news over a shot of Jack Daniels with a Miller Light chaser than it is to be outside taking part in life, nor are fishing and eight-ball the most ambitious of pursuits. He lived in a world that had been left behind. His obsolete ways were quiet and reflective and they required too much space and too much time for people obsessed with accumulating toys.

On the other hand, the enjoyment and dedication he brought to his arts were the very things that made them worthwhile, and they were probably the reasons he insisted on such seriousness when he drank. He certainly repeated the cliche, "A thing worth doing is worth doing well," many times, both in seriousness and in jest. If he didn't also say, "if it ain't worth doing, don't do it," then I imagine I knew him well enough to assume he would have said it if he had thought of it when somebody was around to listen, even if it was only Santoni. I feel sure he would have defended his opponent's right to behave as he pleased, but he always seemed to hope that Santoni and everybody else would choose to act sensibly instead of running around as though they were oversized children with too much money. Perhaps, just as I see the old man as a sort of victim of progress – in that he was unable to adjust to a quickly changing world – he saw most younger people as victims, too, since they adopted the hollow conventions of progress without sufficient thought, restraint or dignity.

How one finally judges whether the old man spent a worthwhile life depends on their outlook on progress. I often found myself reflecting on this issue the day after a contest session. Drinking is certainly an escape but, if the thing to be escaped is irksome enough, perhaps that sort of declaration of independence from the bitter progress of our digitally-fixated world is justifiable. Some fruits of progress are sweet – though even the most advanced medicine was not enough to save the old man from his own habits – but the cost to the old ways of life is great. From my vantage point at the time it was easy to condemn the army of go-getters crashing forward in their Seadoos and Scions. Certainly the old man never wanted to have anything to with them.

Part One

One

The contest began on St. Patrick's Day, caused by the accident of the two men being in the same bar at the same time, and the presence of green beer. Aldridge's favorite place a few blocks away, the Liberty Inn, had been sold to new owners who had raised the drink prices, and he and the other old-timers scattered to taverns throughout the city trying to find a place where they could drink without loud music or a bunch of kids hanging around. The first meeting was in the beginning of this period when a few of them were spending afternoons at the Eight-Ball. It was a wet, gray spring day, so in spite of the early hour, many of the booths and all the seats at the bar were filled.

Aldridge was sitting at a table with me, watching the four pool tables and drinking his trademark bourbon with a small beer chaser. I faced him. One of his older friends sat in a third chair, smoking and nodding at the occasional skilled shot. We were debating the best way to fish for whitefish at Grand Marais in the autumn when Bob Santoni, in town on business, happened by and heard our discussion. He invited himself in and sat down in the empty fourth chair. We compared notes on various fishing methods for about an hour.

Against Santoni's point that it was best to fish from a boat and follow the schools of fish as they moved toward shore, the old man gradually came around to agree with my opinion that it was better to remain stationary on the pier and wait for the fish to pass by.

About an hour later we began shooting eight-ball. Three or four of Aldridge's cronies showed up. Soon we had a real drinking party going. A few small bets were placed on the outcome of the games. Sometime around six, Aldridge passed that magic line of drunkeness that allowed him to concentrate fully on his game and he held the table for the next hour and a half. After being beaten three or four times, Santoni appeared to be getting angry. He stayed seated on one of the tall stools by the wall, veiled in a haze of cigarette smoke, while I lost a game of last-pocket. Later, he returned to the table and said to the old man, "If you could drink like you shoot pool, you would really be something."

In response, Aldridge took a sip of beer and told this story: "I went up to Engadine for the smelt run last year with Big Jon

Kolehouse. We stopped in Pinconning for cheese and beer because we finished the case we bought when we left Washtenaw Lanes. In Mackinaw City we bought two more cases. I counted seven hawks, thirteen turkey buzzards and twenty-three deer between the bridge and Engadine and it started to rain just as we got to Jon's cabin.

"Now, over the course of that weekend we caught enough smelt to fill the back of Jon's brother's pickup truck, and we drank eleven cases of beer. That's over fifty beers a day each, from Friday afternoon to Sunday night."

He eyed Santoni as the story sank in.

"What did you say your name was?" he asked.

Santoni mumbled some response and they continued to size each other up for the next hour. The bartender finished his shift and came over to play me in a few games of pool. Returning to the table between shots, I noticed that both men had switched to the special St. Patty's Day green beer and that one of the other old timers was keeping track of the number of drinks.

I had had one or two by this time and I can remember feeling, through a haze of alcohol, smoke and music, that this challenge was going to be a grand spectacle of age and experience against youth and enthusiasm. I had drunk enough times with

Aldridge to know that, even if his story had been an exaggeration, there were few people who could match him drink for drink, and fewer still who could maintain the kind of dignity he had while drinking that much. I decided that I would write about the contest and publish the installments in the Michigan Daily.

After I sat back down at the table and got another drink, I thought about the characters who would appear in my articles. Aldridge had the small belly and the reddish complexion of a seasoned drinker, and I knew he preferred whiskey and beer. He and his wife lived alone. They had no children. She had been a school teacher for thirty years and, since her retirement, they had lived quietly on their combined pensions.

Santoni would be easy to contrast with Aldridge. His body was still slim, though his belly was beginning to develop, and his face, with its round cheeks that would eventually become imposing jowls, was a pasty white color. Where Aldridge's public manner was dignified and calm, Santoni carried on animated conversations while he drank. Their choice of drinks mirrored their personalities. Santoni preferred mixed drinks or sweet liquor like Southern Comfort. He often talked about his cabin near the Brule River. He owned snowmobiles, skis, boats and motorcycles. At every chance, he would improve the cabin so he could have more guests, tune in more TV channels, or store more cases of

10

beer. In spite of his hyper-enthusiastic personality, he was easy to be around and he had casual friends all over the state.

Aldridge talked quite well, too, when circumstances were right, but his style was different. He always talked about fishing and about traveling around Michigan. He could remember the number of fish caught on a trip thirty years before, as well as conversations he had had with fishermen in almost any good fishing spot we discussed. His personal life otherwise rarely came up.

Two

The first day of drinking at the Eight-Ball set the standard to be followed from then on. The first five or six drinks were a sort of warm up, allowing the two men to size each other up and to coat the linings of their stomachs in preparation for what was to come. Most of the plans for later meetings were made during this time when the contestants were still fairly lucid. At first, I tried to predict the outcome of the matches based on the behavior of each man during this period, but it generally proved to be an inaccurate prediction in Santoni's case. He always began drinking as if he had just emerged from the desert, only to slow later to a more reasonable pace that would allow him to continue for the entire night.

He quickly drank ahead of Aldridge on the night of the green beer. He ordered each early round and swallowed his glass of beer in two or three gulps, until there were five empty glasses in front of him and three full ones before the old man. We had to explain to the waitress the reason for keeping all the glasses on the table, and she indicated that she would require a substantial tip for the inconvenience. For his part, Aldridge continued to consume his drinks at a reasonable pace, getting up to take a shot occasionally and telling me how they used to arrange to get free napkins and paper plates when he worked for Great Lakes Paper.

It seems that the embossed designs on paper products are stamped with big machines. The machines had to be kept very clean because any objects that got on the stamping plates would show up as part of the design on the napkins. The guys at the plant would ask their wives to check on the supply in their pantries at home and, when enough workers needed to restock, they'd get together on a time to take action. Naturally they wanted the company's products to be top quality, Aldridge explained, but could they be blamed for overlooking a tiny wedge of metal now and then, especially since the damaged products were given free to the employees?

While this tale was developing, Santoni had slowed to his marathon drinking pace, which was about equal to Aldridge's. When the total reached about nine drinks, a few of the guys began discussing food. They ordered from the waitress. Santoni ordered a ham and cheese sandwich, but the old man insisted that eating a meal during a round of serious drinking was a mistake. He did nibble a few peanuts, but otherwise kept to his beer and conversation.

As Aldridge finished drink number twelve, we began to lose some of our spectators to drunkenness. The noise level of our group had been gradually increasing as the others tried to keep up, but soon they began to drop out, especially the younger ones. Two or three college students who had been watching decided to find another bar where they could have live music, and one of the old man's cronies had fallen asleep, his head on the table and a thread of saliva descending from his mouth.

At around drink number fifteen, number five for myself, I noticed something that I thought was purely coincidence. Since Aldridge gave no sign of being aware of it, I assumed he was just drinking at his normal pace, but he had gotten one drink ahead and, every time Santoni finished a drink, the old man seemed to be just finishing the one he needed to stay ahead. The color of Santoni's face had changed from its ordinary pasty white to the beginnings of a subtle pink glow. He was getting quieter as time passed and was looking balefully at the old man. I think it was around that time that he realized what he had gotten himself into, and it was also around that time that the rest of us realized that he might actually be able to keep up with Aldridge.

Otherwise the crowd had not thinned out much even though it was approaching midnight. The St. Patty's Day spirit was keeping everybody animated. Groups of people stood around talking and the pool tables were still active, though the quality of play had dropped substantially. I was munching some bread and cheese I had ordered earlier in the evening. The bread had gotten hard and dry, but I wanted something in my stomach to help absorb the awful green beer.

At one forty-five a.m., when the bar closed, the seven of us who remained in the group wandered outside. Two men went a little way down the alley to pee against a wall. The rest of us staggered to our cars. The count since the official start was thirty-two beers for Aldridge, thirty-one for Santoni. I estimated that Aldridge had had at least five whiskeys with a small beer chaser before the contest began. Both men could navigate under their own power.

"That'll be it, then," Santoni was saying, though not too clearly, holding a can of warm Coke he had gotten from the trunk of his car. "The time limit is the closing of the bar."

He let out a loud belch.

Aldridge was silent, moving in short measured steps toward his car. I had promised to drive him to his house on the Old West Side before going home myself.

Three

The second session began on the afternoon of the next day, a Monday. The day was clear and cold and this weather, coming after two weeks of wet spring days, made the atmosphere in the Old Town Bar seem especially convivial. The sun shone through the windows and illuminated the polished woodwork, and the rays of light made paths through the dust and smoke that hung in the air.

The contestants had met at the bar to discuss arrangements for the contest over lunch. By coincidence, J.P. – the one-eyed auto body repair expert from Chelsea – was to pick up the cab I was driving that day so he could repair a front quarter panel. We had agreed to meet at the Old Town for lunch, but because of the lunchtime crowd there were no open tables, and we ended up at the table with the contestants. Both men looked a little tired, but they were eating turkey sandwiches and drinking their trademark drinks, Aldridge his whiskey and beer, Santoni, a Coke. The sun warmed our table. It was a very pleasant, drowsy lunch.

Santoni began telling a story about a fishing adventure he had had near Elsie, at which he and his friends had parked on a bluff overlooking Crescent Lake. The starter on his Oldsmobile failed on the second day of the trip and they were unable to tow the boat down to the lake. One of the friends, who had come up in his own car, drove down to Ann Arbor to pick up his son, a mechanic, to put a new starter on the Olds.

While the friend was en route, the group of five guys who were left stranded walked to a little tavern by the lake. In front of the shack there was an old Olympia Beer sign with the word "Bar" painted over it. That was the name of the place.

While waiting for the friend and his son to return, the group began to play pool and drink Peach Schnapps. What was remarkable about the place was its two pool tables, both so far off level that after the break all the balls would roll back against the far rail and remain there. They had to be shot one by one off the rail, and any that missed the pocket would end up stacked along the rail with the others. What was remarkable about the Peach Schnapps was that these five guys drank all three bottles that the bartender had in the space of the two and a half hours required for the friend to make the round trip to Ann Arbor.

When they had repaired the Olds and gone to the lake, the fishing, Santoni said, had been lousy. At the end of this story, J.P.

and I were nearly asleep, but Aldridge had a glint in his eye that even Santoni noticed.

"They've got that stuff here," the old man said.

So the second round started that day. We had no idea at the time how long the contest was going to run, but it would never again happen that Aldridge would set himself up to drink sweet drinks without being obliged to do so by the rules they set on the first day.

He played it cleverly. After giving Santoni the idea he was silent, but it was easy to see that he wanted to engage the younger man in a bout as soon as possible. He must have been enjoying the sunny weather, because he sat back in his seat and closed his eyes, a weird sort of half smile on his face. It made quite a picture: the smile, the tension he had created when he mentioned the possibility of beginning the second round, the dust motes hanging in the air, and the Tchaikovsky Symphony playing on the stereo.

Santoni took the bait and agreed to begin drinking at once. By doing so, he used up his turn for choosing on a relatively benign sweet drink. Maybe that was what the old man had in mind when he made the suggestion.

Most of the business people were heading back to work. The first round of drinks came and Santoni finished his quickly. The old man sipped his gingerly, complaining that the sugar would stop him before the alcohol. The previous evening's pattern ensued, though more slowly given the early hour. When Santoni had finished six drinks, his opponent had only finished three.

As the sunlight moved to a different set of windows and gradually changed to a deeper golden shade, a different set of people began to drift in. Word had gotten around somehow, and three of the spectators from the night before joined us at the table. Two of them were drinking soft drinks, having attempted to keep up with the action in the first round. J.P. left just before dark with my cab.

The bartender, with whom I had gone to high school, had a dozen Grolsch Lagers in the old style ceramic stopper bottles in the cooler, and had served me two of them deeply cold in mugs taken from the freezer. I saw the old man eyeing the third before I touched it and I offered it to him, knowing what a godsend it would be to have the smooth bitterness of the beer to wash away the taste of the Peach Schnapps.

Santoni stopped in the middle of ordering dinner to caution Aldridge that the beer would not count in his contest drink total. The old man looked silently at him, took up the mug, and drank off half the beer. Afterward I noticed that the half smile was still on his face.

Dinner came, which was Mexican style food, and Aldridge again criticized eating during drinking bouts, especially spicy food. Just as before, he was able to catch up on the drink total while Santoni ate, but this time he was unable to get ahead.

Santoni's strength at drinking sweet drinks was prodigious. He would down a drink in one gulp, between bites of burrito, and calmly go on discussing the merits of various brands of boat motors. One of the spectators, an insurance salesman from Whitmore Lake, was an amateur water skier, so he had a different perspective on the use of such motors than did the old man, who remained silent.

As the night wore on, though, the old man's expression grew less contented and more bitter. He frowned at every statement Santoni made. The color of his face grew slightly gray and I began to worry about his health. The bartender finally brought the last drinks and both men downed them. The evening's drink total stood at twenty-three drinks for Santoni, twenty-one for the old man. We all stood up to go. Aldridge gazed straight ahead in quiet irritation.

"Don't fish for trout in still water," he said on the way out. None of us were sure what he meant.

Four

Nearly two weeks passed before the next session, which took place at Jack's Corner, about eight miles south of Mesick. The service area there was made up of a row of buildings facing M-37, near where the highway intersects U.S. Forestry Service Road Number 5220. The southernmost building was an Amoco station, where Joachim Becker used to repair cars for a decent price. If he couldn't fix your car, he was always happy to sell you one of the junkers he had put together from spare parts. The northernmost building was a combination general store, tourist trap, and diner.

I had nearly frozen the night before while sleeping in the reclined front seat of Santoni's brother's Subaru Outback, parked on the east bank of the Little Manistee River. The brother, Rich, and his friend Matt had nearly frozen too, though they weren't as stiff since they had stretched out in the back, but the cold and uncomfortable accommodations explained why we were in the diner having cup after cup of hot coffee at six thirty in the morning. It didn't explain why there should be anyone there to serve us at that ungodly hour, why the place was half full, or why Aldridge showed up at six forty-five looking as spunky as a sixteen year-old kid, ready to do battle that afternoon.

"Couldn't sleep," was all he said to explain, taking his coat off and hanging it on the back of the empty fourth chair at our table, "so I decided to drive over." He sat down.

He and his wife were staying at their place near Traverse City. They alternated between there and their home in Ann Arbor at random, it seemed, though Aldridge had said that the system for determining where to go was based on his wife's calculations. These calculations included such factors as when her relatives could visit, the timing of good garage sales, and whether or not the garden in either yard needed work. He was just as happy in either place, he said, though of course the best thing was to be out fishing.

The old man's good spirits at that hour of the morning were almost too much to bear, especially since the three of us had stayed at the local tavern – situated between the diner and the Amoco station – until closing time, drinking Tequila Sunrises and shooting nine-ball. We had held a sort of contest among ourselves with those horrible drinks and the two friends had tied with eleven apiece against my seven.

Matt had a gift for sinking the first eight balls, then missing the crucial nine-ball shot, and he wouldn't give up until the place closed. Even at that, he had only won three out of our thirty-seven games. Rich's wallet was the one that had benefited most from Matt's misfortune, but I hadn't done all that badly myself until we played a few games of high stakes backgammon in the Subaru before going to sleep. I ended up about even for the night.

The three of us huddled over our coffee and listened as Aldridge talked about the DNR's program to reintroduce moose to northern Michigan. The waitress came by to bring him a cup of coffee and take his order. She smiled at him.

"Hi Russ," she said, "It's a bit early in the year for trout fishing, isn't it?"

"Yeah Lois. I just drove down here to keep an eye on these young folks. How are the kids?"

They talked a while and he ordered oatmeal. He stirred a little cream in his coffee and the table was quiet for a moment when she walked away.

"They released about seven of 'em around here in the past year," he began to explain about the moose. "I saw one crossing a fire trail when I was up here fishing last summer. They're big bastards.

"What the DNR doesn't realize is that a moose thinks nothing of walking a hundred miles or more in a day. It's nice to have 'em here, but they'll just walk north if the food runs out or if there are too many hunters during deer season. Our tax dollars may fund an increase in Canada's moose population."

"What about the wolves?" Rich asked in spite of beginning to look rather green around the gills as a result of breakfast and his hangover from the night before. "Didn't they release some wolves in the U.P.?"

"Got shot, most of 'em," Aldridge said. "They don't have the natural cunning of the native wolves up there."

"What do you mean?" Matt asked. "I thought there weren't any more wolves in the U.P."

There was no answer at first. The waitress came by to warm up our coffees. She smiled at the old man, but he was staring out the window. The metallic sound of falling silverware issued from the kitchen. Nobody spoke until she was gone.

"I thought there weren't any wolves in the U.P.," Matt repeated.

"Hah!" spat Aldridge. "You and a lot of other people. You need to pay more attention to things. The old timers know."

He leaned toward us conspiratorially and lowered his voice.

"There might even be a few left in the lower peninsula if you look in the right places. Those who watch and listen, learn."

He then went on to tell us about a lake trout planting experiment by the DNR that had failed. It seems that lake trout return to the area where they were born every year. The DNR thought that, by planting a bunch in good fishing spots in the Great Lakes, they could improve the sport fishery. They were hoping the lakers would start spawning in those locations and perpetuate great deep-water fishing. The Native Americans warned them that the trout needed very particular conditions to reproduce, such as gravel bottoms at a certain depth and the right water temperature, but the DNR went ahead and planted them anyway, inflated by their success with the planting of Pacific salmon.

A few of the lakers returned, but most ended up joining other schools that spawned in the original locations. Out of ten thousand or so, something like a dozen were reported caught in the areas that had been planted.

"Got to listen to the Indians," he said after finishing his oatmeal.

Then, having received almost no response to his story, he peered across the table at us.

"You boys okay?" he asked.

We explained how we had spent the evening and he nodded. He reiterated his contention that sweet drinks were the bane of all serious drinkers.

"Anyway, I'm going to take a drive out to the mouth of the Manistee and have a look at the lake," he said. "Anybody want to go along?"

Rich and Matt decided to try to get more sleep in the back of the Subaru, but I agreed to go along for the ride. I couldn't face the thought of trying to sleep in the front seat again, and a ride with the old man would be a good way to get more material for my articles. We confirmed the time of the drinking contest later in the day and the old man pushed his chair back to stand up. As I paid the bill, I watched him walk across the restaurant toward the door. He seemed ageless, striding along with none of the infirmities of old age. He held the door for a young couple before going out, absently nodding a greeting to them. When I had gotten my change and left the tip, I followed him, more slowly, outside.

We set out in his wife's Buick, he driving while I slouched in the passenger seat watching the pine scrub blur past. When we crested a hill, I could see the tall stacks of the natural gas refinery to the north, waste gases being consumed at the top of the stacks by large flames. The old man chattered on, oblivious to the sour pain in my stomach and the dull, throbbing ache I felt at each temple. I kept quiet, knowing he would be experiencing such symptoms himself all too soon.

Five

On the drive back from the mouth of the Manistee, the old
man decided to stop in and look over some of the swampy
drainage areas of the river. He claimed an amateur's interest in
the growth patterns of pine trees and there had been massive
plantings in the area a few years before. The new trees were meant
to replace those that had been removed by logging, but different
varieties were being introduced, and he wanted to see how they
were catching on under these conditions.

At the lake, at first, he had been energetic, walking quite
rapidly out to the shore and showing me how to note the progress
of the wind by observing the surface of the lake. However, he
soon became introspective in the cold air. We stood for a long
time just staring out at the water, alone together on the sand in the
morning light.

Lake Michigan always seemed tamer than Lake Superior up
north. Looking across Lake Superior I always felt its presence and

great weight, and the mystery of what lay to the north. At night, the cold wind and northern lights made me wonder about freezing to death. I had never told anyone of that romantic idea, as it had been acquired in childhood, inspired by the sight of a whitefish frozen into crystal clear ice atop the pier at Grand Marais. It was more wonder than fear – the whitefish was just an example of the power of nature at work. In contrast, Lake Michigan's warmth and unimposing waves made it seem like a big resort lake.

The old man's mouth worked reflexively, his eyes narrowed, and he hummed a few notes from an unrecognizable song. As we stood there, I shivered and regretted not returning to my sleeping bag, but he seemed not to be much affected by the cold. As he grew more and more quiet, an aura of calmness surrounded him, and the dignified old master of the drinking table gradually replaced the talkative instructor he had been all morning. I could feel him gathering strength for the contest later in the day.

It was strangely moving to be with him during that time. I had the sense that he was somehow gaining power from the lake. There was a deep connection between him and the natural surroundings. Looking past him toward the land, I saw his frame outlined against the trees on the distant horizon. The movement of his thinning hair reminded me of the leaves of elm trees fluttering in the wind, the bulking of his jacket of the sudden rush of a covey of quail breaking cover. And there was the steadfast bronze of his aged skin, wrinkled but still supported by good bone structure. Instead of the half smile he had worn during the last drinking bout, his lips were pursed in pre-contest meditation.

When he turned his head suddenly toward me, his eyes were fixed on a distant point on the horizon.

"The wind off the big lake is better," he stated in a monotone. "It comes from farther north."

At the river drainage he showed me how to identify various types of pine trees and to recognize the new growth. The spruce trees, which were only three feet high, were the same age as the seven-foot tall red pines or the nine-foot white pines, he said. To prove this we counted the growth segments on each type and there were, in fact, the same number on most of them, though some had been damaged by snow in previous years.

The whole area was covered by these young evergreens, having been totally logged off a decade before. The absence of large trees gave the landscape the same look and feel as the bush regions farther north where few trees grew tall because of the short growing season and constant cold. Nearer the river, however, there were a few deciduous trees, many with huge broken sections that lay piled up on the marshy ground. We had to pick our path carefully to avoid the holes caused by drainage through the wet soil.

I remembered fishing this river as a child and told the old man about the methods we had used to try to catch browns and brook trout. My father and I would wade upstream in the late afternoon, casting flies or night crawlers until nearly dark, then reverse direction and let the bait drift downstream as we made our way back toward camp. It was not uncommon to hook thirty or forty trout in an evening. It was also not uncommon to be eaten alive by mosquitoes, but that had always seemed to be a fair price to pay for the privilege of such great fishing.

"Fried up a few of those brookies when you got back to camp, did you?" the old man mused. He scanned the water as if imagining our progress along the streambed. The cold water made almost no noise as it slid by. Gradually the chill of the air materialized into a misty rain.

"Good method," he finally pronounced. "We better get back before it really starts raining."

Six

Rich and Matt were at the tavern when we walked in at about two thirty. Santoni and a couple of his salesman friends were there too, already shooting eight-ball. The vivid artificial green felt of the pool table, brightly lit, had a surreal quality after the morning we had spent in the severe early spring landscape. The far corners of the bar receded into the darkness. Besides our group, there were no other customers in the bar. Everyone greeted the old man, but by now he had retreated fully into his tactical reticence.

"How about a sandwich?" he asked me. We sat at the counter to eat and he drank coffee with his chicken sandwich and minestrone soup. Since he stared straight ahead without talking, I swung around on my stool after finishing my cheeseburger to watch the eight-ball action.

Santoni occasionally shot a good game, but he generally played too quickly to set up his shots well. The salesman friend against whom he was playing postured with his cue, strutted back and forth from his seat to the pool table, shot quickly and with too much force, and nearly always missed. He was drinking Bloody Marys.

There were many of his type to be found in the bars. They were men who lived unsatisfying lives at home and who escaped with weekend trips and alcohol, but they generally had no understanding of the unspoken rules of outdoorsmen and serious drinkers. They mainly came along to get drunk and to publicly regret the absence of women, though I saw their complaints as attempts to demonstrate a masculinity they did not actually possess. They could be characterized by their hopeless pool playing, their too loud voices, the creases in their outdoor clothing, and their inability to handle the taste of strong drink. Though Aldridge and his friends disliked them, such men did serve a purpose. They were the court jesters, the ones who made the serious folk look even more exceptional, who could be counted on to lose money at the pool table and perpetually fail to catch fish.

Santoni fell loosely into this category, but he seemed to be working his way out of it. His relative youth provided an excuse for some of his behavior, and he was gradually shooting a better game of pool as time went on. Then, too, the contest brought him into the old man's circle and that automatically invested him with a certain prestige.

With this small crowd of seven men, the session was called to order. We gathered at the largest table in the place, where all of us sat facing one another. One of Santoni's friends began to drum on the table with his fingers, but he was quickly silenced by a glance from the old man. With the gentle clinking of glasses from behind the bar and the drone of daytime television, the atmosphere was appropriately solemn for the ascetic choice Aldridge was about to make.

"Jack Daniels," he said.

There was a moment of silence when we all looked at Santoni for his reaction. He sat for a moment, looking grim. Then, after heaving a huge sigh, he tilted his head in mock pain and let out a sorrowful groan. It looked dark for him, since the old man hadn't had even one drink yet and he would be playing with home field advantage. He put out a hand toward Aldridge.

"Small beer chasers?" he pleaded.

"Won't count," the old man said. "Maybe next time."

If all the sessions had gone as this one went, the old man would have destroyed Santoni in a few days. He radiated strength and confidence during the first half-dozen drinks, while his junior opponent cringed before taking each one. Santoni's face soon took on an ashen pallor and his lips looked drawn and dry. At this stage he looked so bad I idly considered what steps we would have to take if he collapsed. Bourbon was clearly not good for him.

The atmosphere remained tense throughout the evening. Rich and Matt started shooting nine-ball again, and this time Matt played with a grim concentration that took all the fun out of the game. He carefully plotted each shot, taking time to plan the leave and meticulously chalking his cue. Even so, he continued losing. Rich, who was playing apologetically, rarely needed to take more than two shots to win a game. I knew Rich wouldn't throw any games intentionally, but I kept hoping Matt would give up and spare us all the pain of watching him get flayed.

Santoni was playing backgammon against one of his friends, but his concentration was on the drinking game. He steeled himself for each drink. Just before drinking, he would take two or three huge breaths, relaxing his body and preparing for the harsh taste of the whiskey. He would then pick up the shot glass, swallow the contents, slam the glass on the table, and quickly follow it with a sip of Coke. His face would contort. He waited as long as he could after each one, constantly looking up from the board to the old man's glass to check his progress, not taking up the next drink until absolutely necessary.

The old man was so relaxed that he even read the newspaper for a while. He seem to forget about his opponent and the rest of us. He just sat, reading, humming to himself and sipping at his whiskey, finishing one after another in a steady progression. Around dark he ordered a bottle of Heineken and a glass and drank the entire beer in one draft. After that, he looked around as if seeing the rest of us for the first time, smiled, blinked a few times, and asked, "Shoot a game, anybody?"

Santoni, who had been expending great amounts of energy in simply keeping his frustration controlled, almost exploded. His face became beet red and he swore to himself. He downed the drink that sat on the table in front of him and immediately signaled for another.

"I'll play you, old man," he said, his voice thick with emotion.

They got up from the table staring at one another like boxers before a match. Aldridge was the old master, with the light of wisdom in his eyes and a smug half smile that seemed to mock the younger player. Santoni was the young challenger, convinced of his own powers and not at all satisfied that the reputation of a man more than twice his age should so entirely eclipse his own. The old man had dominated him so fully today that his competitive spirit was starting to overcome even his distaste for the awful whiskey. He wanted not only to beat the old man at the drinking table but also at pool, at the backgammon board, and even at fishing if that were possible.

Of course it would be years before Santoni enjoyed the kind of drinking and fishing authority Aldridge possessed. Even if he managed to eventually win the drinking contest, there was little hope that his reputation would grow large enough to fill the old man's shoes. What he had now was the strength of youth and the drive to win. He'd need these and a lot of luck to win the contest. He'd need thirty-five years of experience to equal his opponent at the larger game of life.

But he was having no luck at the pool table even though he was shooting far above his ordinary level, actually sinking bank shots and getting great leaves. Aldridge was so much on in every area that, whenever Santoni made even the least mistake, he took over and simply dropped balls into the pockets until he had won another game. He continued to sip his way through one Jack Daniels after another.

Now that Santoni had committed himself to the drinking, however, he was keeping up fairly well. He made less of a fuss before each drink and there were moments when he actually seemed to be enjoying the combat. How much of this was a psychological ploy to intimidate the old man, how much pure competitive spirit, and how much advanced drunkenness, was not clear.

The final hour of drinking was a pressurized head-to-head session that drove one of the salesmen right out of the bar to be sick. The two contestants sat across from one another and stared straight at one another. The old man had a margin of five drinks by this time and he was just coasting, waiting for Santoni to make a move. Santoni was visibly struggling for control of his drunken body. He picked up his shot glass and downed a drink. In response, the old man picked up his glass, tilted it slightly against his lips, and sucked the contents slowly into his mouth. He then swallowed so extravagantly that the taste of bourbon must have penetrated every pore of his tongue and throat. Santoni's friend, who had been sitting heavily and watching the action, jumped up and dashed out the front door, knocking his chair over in the process. He was still standing outside in the cold air when we left.

Santoni made a most valiant effort. As closing time approached, he drank more and more rapidly. His movements became more and more erratic, but he was managing to get the awful brown liquid into his stomach. Nobody else had been drinking for the past hour and, on an otherwise empty table, there were finally three full shot glasses in front of Santoni and one in front of Aldridge. Aldridge sat and watched his opponent struggle against nausea, dizziness and fatigue without touching his own drink. Santoni finished one and, just before two o'clock, another. When the second hand swept up to point directly at the twelve, Aldridge picked up his glass and drained it.

"That's it, then," he said.

Santoni stared at him dumbly. It looked as though he wasn't even going to be able to pick up his last drink. While the rest of us stood, he continued to sit. Could this be the end already? I wondered.

Then the younger man drank. He tilted his head back and dumped the drink into his open mouth. After swallowing, his eyes glazed over. He sat gazing ahead with a sheen of whiskey on his lips. We waited for him to stand. Looking ready to pass out, he was somehow able to rise and begin tottering toward the door.

He teetered and weaved horribly, just managing to move forward, and had to make three tries before getting hold of the door knob. But he was alive and had not conceded the game. We filed after him in a solemn procession. The old man, getting into the passenger seat of his wife's car, was silent and calm. The final count of the sessions was thirty-four whiskeys for Aldridge and thirty-one for Santoni.

Seven

Two more weeks passed before the next session. Naturally, after the strong showing by the old man, Santoni wanted to stage a comeback. He had chosen the Black River Tavern in Black River, a town otherwise known only for its annual festival celebrating the deer tick. The event took place every July, but fortunately we were going to miss it.

The tavern, which had once been a quiet place for old timers to drink, smoke and sit without talking, had recently been redecorated in a sports theme complete with a big screen TV, baseball banners, and a giant stuffed tiger whose eyes lit up while the head moved back and forth. There was neon lighting in excess and the music choices tended toward rock. Aldridge hated the place.

Luckily for him it was very quiet on this Saturday evening. It was still early May and though the weather was beginning to get warm, there were still very few tourists in town. The regular crowd that had come here before the remodeling had escaped to other, quieter locations on the outskirts of town. The old man was uncomfortable in strange crowds and preferred to be surrounded by his own group. If the place had been packed, on top of it being Santoni's night to choose, Aldridge might have fared very badly, indeed.

Santoni had gone to great lengths to shift the power balance in his favor. Besides the two salesman friends of his who had attended the last session, he had brought along a young water skiing champion who was on a tour of Michigan promoting a new brand of skis, and the skier's sister, a lovely woman without a hint of intelligence in her eyes.

This abundance of youth and vapidity was a counterweight against our group: Rich, Matt, myself, and Big Jon Kolehouse, the Chippewa Indian friend of Aldridge's who was famous for prodigious drinking in his own right. In any single session, Jon could have easily out drunk either contestant, since he outweighed even Santoni by at least one hundred pounds and never appeared even the least bit drunk regardless of how much alcohol he consumed. He was not regarded as a serious drinking threat, however, because he often passed out in the middle of drinking sessions and slept sitting up for ten or twelve hours. With this solid backing of tradition for Aldridge, Santoni's advantage was questionable, but the environment and the choice of drinks was definitely in his favor.

"Yukon Jack," he announced when everyone was sitting.

"Gar!" ejaculated the old man. "That stuff's drain cleaner."

Santoni grinned an idiotic grin and rubbed his belly. Only his salesmen friends laughed. The old man's glare silenced the rest.

All ten of us were assembled around two tables on a sort of raised indoor deck at the far end of the bar. Drinks were ordered. The two contestants faced one another at one table with Big Jon and Rich occupying the left and right sides to keep track of the drink total. Matt started out sitting kitty corner to one of the salesmen, with a backgammon board between them. The other salesman faced the water skier, pouring adulation over him while ogling the sister, with whom I was left sitting.

She had a nice Scottish face and unruly reddish brown hair, but stood a head taller than I. She was very outgoing and smiled and leaned toward me as we talked. Even the old man looked over the first time she spoke. Her voice was low and sexy and she used it well. The things she said, however, did not inspire much confidence in her ability to reason or to calculate vectors for interplanetary travel by rocket.

As the drinking progressed, I glanced at the other side of the table from time to time to see how things were going. Santoni was staying about two drinks up and the old man was looking unhappy. Rich was babbling away about a new trout stream he had found near Traverse City, and Big Jon was silently matching the contestants drink for drink. The sister sipped ginger ale and leaned toward me.

"I hear you're pretty smart," she said. I shrugged.

"You have a college degree, right?" she persisted, tapping the table in time with her words with long, pink fingernails. Not wanted to be rude, I smiled and nodded.

"So you must be smart. What degree did you get?"

I may have been drinking on an empty stomach, because I was flattered by her attention. Her laughter was low and pleasant and it provided moments when I could look at her face without seeming to stare.

"Got broke," I said. "Tuition long time many paying."

"C'mon, seriously."

"Really broke no wampum," I said. She looked at me impatiently. I gestured toward Jon.

"Ask heap big red man. Many moon white man pay. Tatonka no come. Squaw no come. Long time dry crow many eating."

"Cut the shit," Jon said, his face expressionless.

After managing to find out that I had gone to graduate school, she wanted to know what I was doing with my life. She was wide eyed with sincerity and touching concern for my well being. I avoided her questions in two or three ways, but she finally insisted on an answer and I admitted that I was driving a cab and going along on these adventure of drinking and fishing. She sat back, serious.

"I think it's terrible," she announced, "that you're not doing anything more valuable with your life. You could be accomplishing so much, but instead you sit here drinking yourself sick along with this poor old man."

"She's really got our number," I said to Jon.

"Not mine," he said.

Rich was still prattling on about the new trout stream.

"KA-CHONG!" he said, to dramatize a strike by some particularly enormous fish. "ZING! That sucker zipped out of there. Man! But I know where he holes up, now."

It seems there were various methods for telling a fish story.

"Mister Santoni is going to feel left out," I said to the nice lady. "What about him? Can't you offer up your appraisal of him as well?"

"But look at everything he's doing," she said. "He's got a nice home, a summer place with satellite TV, two cars, snowmobiles. And he never even went to college."

Her defense of Santoni caused a few smiles among those in our group. I caught a wink from the old man. She continued with much drama. "Anyway, he's going to quit drinking. As soon as this contest is over, he said."

This was such a patent lie that everybody at both tables burst out laughing, including Santoni himself. Luckily, Big Jon's back was between her and the object of her admiration. It wasn't clear if she, wide eyed and righteous, understood that she was being laughed at. I selected this moment to extricate myself.

"White girl speak with forked tongue," I said. "Heap big red man settum straight. Anybody wanna shoot a game?"

"Cut the shit," Jon repeated, deadpan, but he turned to talk to the girl. Matt agreed to play a game of nine-ball. He had won seven games of backgammon in a row, and almost a hundred dollars, and he was getting bored. I set up the nine balls and selected a cue from the rack on the wall. Matt sank the four ball on the break and missed a shot on the one. I missed the same shot and went to take a sip of my beer.

To take his mind off the taste of the Yukon Jack, the old man asked Rich to play backgammon. At nine drinks for him and ten for Santoni, he was beginning to look tired. Santoni, as usual, was unfazed by the sweetness of the drinks and actually tilted each glass back to get the last tasty drops of liquor off the ice cubes. Aldridge dutifully finished each drink to stay close to his opponent.

By this stage in the contest, both men had already become accustomed to drinking the huge amounts. They would be dazed by the end of the sessions but, in the middle hours, between the ten and twenty drink range when most men would already have been completely drunk, neither showed many signs of intoxication. While the spectators and score keepers around them would pass through various phases of silliness, finally lapsing into drunken stupors near the end on less than half the number of drinks consumed by the contestants, the two men would be concentrated and alert for any sudden moves by their opponent.

These moves consisted mostly of one opponent's decision to speed up or slow down his drinking in the hope that the other would either fail to keep up or drink too quickly and end up losing control. Santoni, being the younger and more reckless of the two, usually initiated these moves. Aldridge's response was to continue his steady drinking on the assumption, almost always correct, that Santoni would, in the case of his speeding up too much, have to slow down later or risk losing consciousness. The old man was much better at being able to unbalance his opponent by exuding confidence even as he deliberately stalled while Santoni was speeding up, or by calmly finishing each drink a moment after the other man finished his own, whatever the pace. Santoni would sometimes make faces at the old man, growl at him, or try to upset the backgammon board to throw him off balance. He was usually ignored.

This night was unusual in that the old man had decided to have a bite to eat during the match. The others had finished their meals by the time his cheeseburger and coleslaw arrived. Since he was concentrating on his backgammon game and trying to ignore his opponent's cheerful attempts to slide their table away from him, he left the cheeseburger sitting on its plate.

"It's too hot now," he said. He watched Santoni slurp down a drink and quickly swallowed his own.

"Ick," he said, looking back at the board for his next move. Santoni was staring at him, his eyes intent, looking for an opening. His eyes bored into the side of the old man's head. I moved to the far side of the pool table so I could watch Matt's attempt to sink the nine ball. He had a simple shot since the ball was flush with the rail but in a good position to be sliced down to the corner pocket, so it looked like he was actually going to win one. He bent over the table and slid the cue back and forth in preparation.

Just then Santoni, who had become exasperated with his failure to distract the old man, shot out his hand and grabbed his opponent's cheeseburger. He took a solid, vindictive bite out of it and returned it to the plate. Everyone else was stunned, waiting for the old man to explode. Matt, disturbed by the sudden silence, muffed his shot.

"God dammit!" he choked. He had left me a perfectly straight shot into the corner.

Since nobody dared laugh at Aldridge, they all erupted into laughter at Matt's outburst. Smirking, Santoni thoroughly chewed the bite of cheeseburger before swallowing it, content that he had finally gotten to the old man. I couldn't help but grin as I sank the nine ball. Matt looked ready to cry.

Aldridge's expression had softened into a vague stare. Without lifting his eyes from the backgammon table he picked up his next drink and finished it, then lifted the damaged cheeseburger to his mouth and took a leisurely bite. He chewed it while thoughtfully considering his next move. He got a good roll of the dice and sent two of Rich's stones to the bar. Santoni's gambit had entirely failed.

Big Jon vanished around one o'clock. We found him later sleeping in the front seat of his dark green Suburban. Somehow by this time the water skier's sister had ended up sitting next to Aldridge telling him her worries in a serious, confiding voice. The old man kept her going by nodding occasionally and making sympathetic noises.

"What a nice old man," she said as we were leaving. Her brother was telling one of the salesmen how he had won the Budweiser Open Trick Ski Competition with an old, outdated ski and the salesman was nodding while keeping his eyes trained on the sister's posterior. The old man, getting into his wife's car, held his belly and shook his head in dismay.

"The devil himself invented those drinks," he said. "Only a damn fool would agree to drink them."

But the gleam had never left his eyes and Santoni had only managed to win by three drinks, despite his best efforts. The evening's total was twenty-nine shots of Yukon Jack for Santoni, twenty-six for Aldridge, and next time it would be the old man's turn to choose. As the weather warmed up, it looked like there was going to be some hard drinking ahead.

Eight

The following Saturday, a group of six people, including myself, arrived at Louie's bar in Traverse City. We filled two booths under the famous moose, near the pool tables. There was a baseball game on the television, and a group of teenagers stood around one pool table watching as their friends missed shot after shot. The early afternoon crowd was small but noisy.

I went up to the bar to order drinks. As I waited for the bartender to finish making our drinks, I happened to look to my right, and there was Aldridge sitting at the bar. An empty shot glass and a half filled beer sat in front of him on the counter, as well as a bowl of Louie's famous chili. A handful of oyster crackers was softening in the chili. The old man was sitting with his shoulders hunched forward, staring straight ahead at the rows of bottles behind the bar with no expression on his face.

"How's the fishing?" I asked.

He turned toward me and stared for a moment before coming out of his reverie. Then he recognized me.

"Damn bad," he said. Streams are too crowded these days."

He smiled and we shook hands. He invited me to sit down, but the drinks were ready, so I told him that the others were waiting over in the booths. He looked a little confused when I mentioned the others, but said he would be over as soon as he finished his meal.

I took the drinks over to the group and sat down with them.

"The old man's already here," I said.

"Is he ready?" Santoni asked.

"Dunno. He's just sitting there with his lunch."

Fifteen minutes or so passed before Aldridge joined us.

"Damn crowded," he repeated, setting his drinks on the edge of one of the tables. Everyone looked up and there was a chorus of greetings, but the old man just scowled and slid onto the seat next to Rich. The others were waiting for their lunches to arrive and there was an excess of horseplay going on. Now and then a package of oyster crackers or a book of matches would come sailing over the back of the seat to land on our table or on someone's lap. Tim, who owned a knife store in Lansing, started hugging Santoni, who threatened to report the behavior to Tim's wife. They were giggling like schoolgirls.

Aldridge looked over at me with one raised eyebrow. "You came with these children?"

Things settled down a bit after the lunches arrived and the old man started telling a story about fishing for northern pike in Lake Superior with his cousins from Wisconsin.

"Goddamn water skiers," he began, "have got no feeling for other people on a lake. You know where the river is damned up near Saxon, on the other side of the Indian reservation? Well, the perch are a damn sight easier to find in there than out on the big lake, so we went out in the morning to catch bait. Those sons a bitches buzzed around us two or three times. Pretty cold to go around half naked. Didn't scare the perch – they're too stupid – but we were rocking back and forth like crazy. Otherwise, the water was smooth as glass.

"After zipping around the lake all morning the horses asses decided to come over and say hi. 'How's the fishing?' they said."

Everyone muttered at the stupidity of the water skiers and Santoni started to explain that he was always very careful not to disturb the fishermen when he went skiing, but Aldridge would have none of it.

"So we had our bait," he interrupted, "and we hauled the boat back into Ashland. After breakfast, we launched from that little marina by the Bayside Hotel and rode out to fish the breakwaters.

"Anyway, at twelve-oh-one it was time to get out the beer, of course ..."

"Of course," Rich echoed.

"... and we started listening to a Badgers game on the radio. Now, my cousins still fish northerns in the old way, with great big rods and floats to keep the perch off the bottom. They have these thick bamboo rods I remember using as a kid. Well, we got so we weren't paying much attention to the rods, what with the game being close and all, I guess it was the Spartans they were playing that day, and it must have been a couple of hours before we realized that two of the floats were down."

"'How long they been down?' I asked, and my cousin Bill says, 'Long enough!' and yanks back on one of the rods just as cousin Greg is saying, 'Wait!'"

He paused a moment to make sure everyone was following the story. The waitress came to clear away the mass of empty plates and bowls.

"Well, Bill comes up with nothing but the float and the perch, but here's the thing of it. The thing of it was, that perch had been scaled, almost up to the head.

"Now, you may think the great northern pike is a vicious predator and that he just grabs his dinner and gulps it down, and you may be right, but I'm here to tell you that when he has the leisure, he scales those babies clean before he eats 'em. Don't ask me how. Maybe he holds the tail between his teeth and just works that baby inward. Spits out the scales and just swallows the rest, eh?

"So we waited another twenty minutes on that other float, with Greg going on about how they always waited half an hour for the fish to scale the bait before they tried to set the hook, and what had gotten into Bill anyway? Bill apologized and said that with the excitement of the football game and all he had just gotten carried away. Greg sat down and opened another beer and we listened until the end of the third quarter before he said to me, 'Go ahead and hit him.'"

Aldridge paused to take a sip of whiskey, then he blew out a long breath of air before following up the whiskey with half his beer chaser. Everyone in both booths was following his story, having mostly finished their lunches, and they were silent while he recovered his voice. He shook his head and leaned back against the seat before continuing.

"I was younger then and I didn't have too much trouble hauling that fat hog into the boat," he laughed. "It went twenty-one pounds on the De-Liar, at about thirty-three inches. And do you know what?"

"What," I responded.

"When we gutted that bastard we found the other perch in his gullet."

"And?" somebody asked.

"And what?" said Aldridge, pretending to look annoyed and finishing his beer. He drank slowly and we could see his old Adam's apple move up and down beneath the wrinkled skin of his neck.

"What about the fucking scales?" Matt said.

"Strangest damn thing," Aldridge said, scratching his head. "Every single scale was still in place."

That broke us up for a little while and soon everybody had a drink and was hollering about something or another. The pool table had opened up and two of Rich's friends who had come over from Alpena went to play. Finally, Santoni looked at the old man and said, "You ready?"

"Ready for what?"

"Today's the twentieth. Drinking. Fifth session, remember?"

Aldridge glared at him for a moment. He looked at me and I nodded. There was suddenly a feeling of tension in the air.

"I wondered what you guys were doing up here," he said. "It's not the twenty-seventh? Next week?"

When we thought back to the week before, everyone who had been there remembered it as the twentieth except Aldridge, but nobody could be sure we had made it clear to him at the time.

"I got nothing against drinking on any particular day, but how about tomorrow?" Aldridge asked, scratching his head again. "I've got to go visiting with the wife tonight, you see."

Allowing for the possibility of error, Santoni agreed that he couldn't force the old man to drink against his will, but he was concerned that this kind of scheduling problem might become a regular thing. Aldridge offered to call his wife and try and rearrange things, but he expected that she had her mind set on that evening to see her friends. Santoni stated that if that's the way it was, then that was the way it was, and finally, out of respect for seniority (and senility, Matt whispered), they postponed the whole thing until the following week.

Driving south that evening, Rich and I discussed the misunderstanding. Bob had stopped off in Acme with a weak excuse about visiting an old friend, with much winking and implication, and it was apparent that he didn't mind the delay too much, after all.

"You think that old fart really just forgot," Rich asked.

"Not much like him, is it," I said.

We drove in silence for a while, watching the sides of the road race past. We were just coming into the part of Michigan where the pines began to give way to more deciduous trees, and the dark green to the lighter set of varied shades of buds about to open. When I had left Ann Arbor the day before, the trees were already substantially in leaf, but up here the season was just getting underway. In the drainage ponds beside the road, the carp were churning the water into a muddy soup.

"Screwing their brains out," Rich said, letting go of the wheel for a moment to make an obscene gesture with his hands. "Like my brother."

"Carp have no brains," I said, "like your brother. He's going to get caught one of these times getting his jollies in the wrong places."

"Did you ever consider," Rich nodded, pondering aloud, "the possibility that Aldridge knew what he was doing all along? That it was just a real clever psychological trick to throw Bob off balance?"

That idea was enough to shut us up all the way past Grayling.

Nine

The Louie's Bar session did take place the following week, and the next four sessions followed in various locations around the state, with the results being more or less as expected each time. The old man won his sessions, and the pressure of drinking so much whiskey began to wear down his opponent. Only when Santoni was able to choose the drinks did he win the day. Though he switched from one strange drink to another in an effort to unnerve the old man, it seemed clear that the greater negative effect was on himself. Aldridge was very steady. His only concession to variety was to occasionally include beer chasers in the total. It was a wild night for him when he elected to drink Heineken chasers instead of the usual Miller Lights.

Perhaps each man was beginning to coast on his off night. Several people wondered whether Santoni was doing his best when the old man won twenty-nine drinks to twenty-three at Louie's, and the same question came up about the old man the next week when Santoni won by five drinks at St. Ignace. The speculation was quiet, however, since none of the rest of us wanted to try to drink as many drinks of either kind as even the loser of these matches.

The most notable of these sessions was the third. The site that had been chosen was a small bar called Zukey Lake Tavern, about half an hour's drive from Ann Arbor. I had driven the late shift the night before while Aldridge defeated Santoni with a margin of five drinks in a quiet session at Frazer's Pub, and was still asleep when J.P. honked his horn from the street below my window. After shouting at him to wait I dressed hurriedly and ran out with my shoes in my hand. He laughed at all this rushing about. He was of the same calm, slow paced school as Aldridge.

The two men had been fishing at Portage Lake the morning before and had taken nearly one hundred pan fish, he told me as he drove. Aldridge landed one perch that went nearly three pounds, close to the state record, and a smallmouth bass that weighed about five.

"Son of a gun out fished me by about two to one," said J.P.. "He always does."

I asked him for his opinion on why Aldridge was such a good fisherman. He shrugged before going on to explain that the old man had grown up around fishermen and had always lived near water.

"It's second nature with him," he said. "After so many years of fishing he just naturally finds the best places to anchor the boat. He knows how deep to fish."

He was silent for a while as we remained stopped at an intersection. He turned onto Mast Road and didn't begin to talk again until we had gotten up to speed.

"He knows what bait to use when, all that stuff. What it is, though, you know what it is?" He looked at me with his one good eye.

"Hm?" I said. "What?"

"He's incredibly patient. That's the main thing."

He had a styrofoam cup half filled with coffee on the dashboard and he took it down to drink.

"You know, all the old farts can shoot a game of pool and drink a few beers, but Russ is just more patient than most. He sets his mind on something and just keeps at it 'till he can do it better than other folks."

A car pulled even with us on the left and tooted its horn. We looked over to see Santoni and his brother waving like idiots and grinning. They had all the windows down and their hair was blowing wildly in the wind. I could hear their radio blasting polka music. We waved and they sped past us, the one-two-three of the music hanging in the air for a moment before changing pitch and then being lost in the other road sounds. J.P. didn't speak again until Santoni's car had vanished around a curve in the road ahead.

"I bet you didn't know I used to work with Russ," he said. I shook my head, not realizing he would miss the gesture. He continued anyway.

"Yup, I worked up there for a while. In those days we used to go out for beers almost every morning after work. We worked the night shift and finished at seven. There was this bar there that opened early for our crowd. Since his wife was gone to teach school daytimes, Russ always stayed there for two or three hours after the rest of us left, shooting pool by himself. After a while it got so nobody could beat him. He had to wait for strangers to come in on the weekends to have anybody to play.

"That's the kind of patience he has. Once he sets his mind on something he just keeps at it and at it. Not too many folks like that around."

J.P.'s admiration for Aldridge was no surprise to me, but I wondered if the kind of patience he described was a trait of all men of his generation. Although he was extremely modest about it, J.P. himself was something of a legend in the area for his great auto body work. I had seen him transform some very worn out cars into brand new looking vehicles in a matter of a few days. The quality of his work, as well as its speed, was far above that of everybody else in the area. In addition to his professional work, he also undertook to repair the cars of his friends. Usually, a couple of beers were enough to satisfy him in return. It must have taken him a few years of hard work to get that good.

When we pulled up to the tavern, nearly all the parking spaces in front were filled. A couple of Ann Arbor townies were leaning against a car, talking loudly to one another and gesturing wildly. They saluted as we walked past. Santoni and his brother were already inside, it seemed, and I recognized many of the other cars as belonging to one person or another from the crowd that had been following these bouts. From the look of things we were going to have quite a party.

The tavern was jumping. It was early afternoon, so the air was still fairly smoke free, but it was otherwise filled with the sounds of country music, talking, shouting and laughter. Every table but one was filled with men who were somehow connected to the drinking game. The only group I didn't recognize was a foursome in a booth near the pool table, a middle aged couple with a younger pair, and I wondered how they were feeling in the midst of all this revelry. They held serve at the pool table but that would probably change soon in the face of our group's enthusiasm and talent at billiards.

The contestants were already seated in a booth midway down the right hand wall. Rich sat with them but the fourth seat was empty, so I walked over to the table.

"Put it on down," the old man said. An oblong plastic basket with some oily white paper and a few tired French fries sat in front of him. There was also a half full glass of beer. The two Santonis' orders hadn't yet arrived.

"I got to go to the head," I said. "What are the drinks?"

"Hasn't been announced yet," Rich told me.

I was suddenly knocked sideways by a clap on the shoulder from Big Jon. He grinned and walked past me toward the men's room. Just then the waitress came up to the table with some drinks and, to get out of her way, I followed Jon toward the back. As I walked past the pool table, the older man in the unfamiliar foursome made a remarkable three rail shot on the eight ball. Perhaps we wouldn't be taking the table away from them as soon as I had thought.

At the urinals Jon and I stood side by side, looking down at the deodorizer cakes.

"What's new, Jon?" I asked. "I thought you were supposed to be up in Newaygo this weekend."

"Yup," he said thoughtfully, "I was. My wife needed the car though, so I decided to come out here instead. I hitched a ride with that Ken guy."

Ken was the name of one of Santoni's more irritating salesman buddies.

"You ever see that girl again?" I asked.

"Which girl?"

"The water skier's sister."

"You mean the one from the Black River trip?"

There was a moment of silence as he made his way back to the sink. While washing his hands he said, "I thought everybody knew. That's Bob's big secret."

"Bob? Santoni?"

"Yup. Why do you think he keeps going up to Traverse City when he's got that cabin on the Brule? She's a camp counselor or something up in Acme."

"Hoo boy," I said, shaking my head. "I hope his wife doesn't find out."

The drink choice had been announced while we were in the men's room. Santoni had chosen Southern Comfort. Aldridge didn't seem too concerned and he was chatting happily with J.P. about the old days at the paper plant.

Santoni, having had an idea of how many people would show up for this session, had actually called ahead and warned the owner of the bar to stock up on Southern Comfort. The owner had brought in two cases of the drink, so almost everybody in our party was drinking double Southern Comforts on the rocks.

"I sort of like this stuff," the old man mused, holding up his glass and watching the light refract through the ice cubes. Santoni, trying to act casual, swallowed and made worried eye contact with his brother. I decided to wait until I had eaten before trying any myself.

A group of men from Ann Arbor Arms, the only gun shop in town, began to sing along with the country hits on the jukebox. They were actually quite good, each singing in a different register, the tall, skinny retail manager harmonizing. Aldridge leaned back in his seat and smiled. I could hear him humming along. In the background was the steady din of voices discussing various drinking methods and the occasional click of billiard balls.

The son of one of Santoni's friends, whose name had come up in one of the fishing tales early on in the contest, had brought along a couple of his friends. They were the youngest people in the place and had decided that the best way to drink large quantities was to get as much as possible down in the shortest time possible. I remembered myself ten years before and the similar mistakes I had made, and Rich and I made a wager on how long they would last. He said they would be gone within two hours, while I predicted that they would last between two and three. It occurred to us that they might not have arranged for anybody to take them home later, so Rich went to make sure someone relatively sober was going to drive.

Meanwhile, a strange scene was unfolding in front of me at the drinking table. For the first time in the contest, the old man was actually keeping up with Santoni's early fast drinking. When J.P. came by to have a look at the scoring tablet – we had started using an old notebook to record the results – he scratched his head and peered at the old man.

"You feeling okay, Russ?" he asked.

The old man gazed at Santoni with his steady eyes and hummed a bit of the refrain from "You Can't Always Get What You Want" by the Rolling Stones. It was all most un-Aldridge-like behavior.

To escape from this steady onslaught of confidence, Santoni went to put a quarter on the pool table. The older man, who was about to shoot, watched Santoni walk up to the table, and continued watching until he had put the quarter down and returned to our booth. Once Santoni sat down, he made his shot.

My two chicken sandwiches arrived and I started to eat. I had decided to have a beer as well and ordered a Molson on draft. It was the first beer of the day and delicious.

The old man swallowed another Southern Comfort and paused before sipping from a beer he was using to cut the sweetness. His brown eyes were thoughtful and distant.

"I was just thinking," he began without any prompting, "about an old friend of mine. I wonder what his wife is doing these days."

Santoni got up to have his turn at the pool table.

"This guy, Steve Bandrovchek, used to turn up all over the state. I remember once when I was driving around the U.P. with another fellow from work and we decided to have a swim in the big lake. This was on that stretch of beach between Grand Marais and Muskallonge Lake. 'Course, this was in August, the hottest part of the year, and I was a little younger then. My buddy used to wear t-shirts with the sleeves cut off all the time and he had the funniest suntan. His belly and chest were as white as you can imagine.

"Anyway, after all that exertion we decided to get a beer, so we drove down to Pine Stump Junction. When we pulled into the parking lot there was this pickup truck with a camper on the back that looked familiar. I kept thinking 'I know that truck,' but I couldn't put it together with anybody who would be there at that time.

"Well, we walk in," the old man went on, looking up at Santoni, who had already returned to his seat, "and there is Steve sitting at the bar with his ladyfriend, Eva. They weren't married then you see. They're just sitting there grinning, happy as mud puppies and already pretty tight, by the look of things.

"'About time you got here,' I said, though of course I had no idea they would be there, and then I notice that John Davis. the owner, is behind the bar and he's looking pretty tight, too. What the hell is going on, I wondered.

"Anyway, me and my buddy sat down and had a few drinks with them, and we talked about all kinds of things, from fishing Portage Lake where Steve had a cottage, to sign painting at the University, which is what Steve did for a living, you see. At some point, of course, I had to go to the john, which I did, and that's when I found out what was up.

"Where until that time they had had a couple of cheap signs, one saying 'men' on the men's room door and one saying 'women,' naturally enough on the ladies room, they now had a couple of real nice paintings. One was a buck and one was a doe, each on the appropriate door with the appropriate lettering beneath it. I could see the paint wasn't dry yet.

"It came out, finally, that Steve had gone in and offered to paint them for free and Davis had accepted the offer but then had decided that he should buy Steve a few drinks to compensate him for his efforts. Somewhere along the way he had decided he should join in the fun as well, I guess. You can see that getting your bathroom doors painted in Pine Stump Junction is a pretty big deal. It was around that point that we came in."

He paused long enough to finish another drink. Santoni, who after the break hadn't even gotten a chance for a second shot, encouraged Aldridge to have a try at the pool table. He offered to put a quarter up on his way to the men's room, and the old man handed him one from the change that sat on the table.

The group of firearms men had stopped singing and were playing cards at their table. People had coalesced into groups at tables and at the bar and we were getting into the early middle period of drinking. Though the jukebox seemed to have been turned up, the general noise level in the place was more steady and composed of mostly calmer voices than before. The kids were still drinking, showing good endurance but not yet having exceeded the range for Rich's prediction.

"The reason I think of it," Aldridge began again, "is that Steve always drank Molson when it was available. He was a good guy.

"Seems they found out he had stomach cancer a few weeks before I ran into him up there. He was taking that stuff, what do you call it? Chemo? And to kill the bad effects he was smoking a lot of pot. But other than that, he was a good guy. We used to do a fair amount of drinking together."

There was a kind of tightness around his eyes that I hadn't seen before. A casual look might have mistaken the expression for a smile, but I could see that it was something else.

"It looked like he was going to pull through for a while. He had surgery a couple times and then he'd be alright for a while. They got married somewhere in there, too. I went to the wedding."

"Table's open," Rich said to him. The old man turned to him and nodded. Sadly, it seemed to me.

"Yeah," he sighed, "he died finally, but he used to show up all over the place. A good guy."

Rich got up to let him stand up and the old man slid out into the aisle. Standing up, he grinned – the eyes hadn't changed and it was as much a grimace as a smile – and shook his head.

"I bet you lunkheads didn't even notice, did you?" He looked at me and over at Jon, who sat in the next booth.

"What?" I said. He waited.

"What?" Jon asked.

"Next time you go to the men's room, take a look at the doors," he said. He went over to the pool table to break.

I finally got my first Southern Comfort and wondered as I drank it how Aldridge could drink so many of them without gagging. The sweetness was nauseating. The beer that he had been sipping must have been more a medical necessity than an indulgence.

"Well, Jon," I said, after finishing the awful stuff. He slid out into the aisle and stood up, towering over me.

Aldridge was shaking hands with the old man at the pool table. I overheard some mention of a certain street in Ishpeming as we passed.

Sure enough, on the doors to the restrooms were two comical monuments to the talents and travels of Aldridge's late friend. The doors were labeled "Geese" and "Ganders," respectively, and above the words were grinning cartoon heads of Canadian geese. The female version had long eyelashes and rather vampy lipstick. It was the fourth or fifth time I had been in the establishment and I had never paid attention to the paintings before. It seemed appropriate that a friend of Aldridge's should have that kind of quiet but quirky memorial.

But the story had cast a shadow on an otherwise pleasant day and I wondered why the old man had told it. He was engaged in a difficult three rail shot on the eight ball when I returned to our table and I studied his face as I walked by. It didn't seem sadder than usual, but I noticed the depth of the lines on his forehead and around his mouth more than I had in the past. Watching him calculate the angles and set up the shot made me realize that he did seem to move slowly, as if carrying a burden or a painful stomach, and that his dignity might have come as much from a deep reserve of sorrow as anything else. Was his absorption with games a method of trying to forget the sadnesses that come with a long life?

He had at last found an eight-ball opponent worthy of his skill. They were playing with a rule that required a three rail shot on the eight, and the other man missed his first attempt by a tiny margin.

They went back and forth with some extraordinary attempts before the other man finally managed to win. Since nobody else was waiting to get on the pool table, they decided to play again. Back at the booth, Rich informed me that the kids were outside being sick. He handed me a nickel. They had lasted two hours, he said, but just barely, and Ken was going to drive them home before heading home to have dinner with his wife. Big Jon could get a ride with one of us.

Santoni was sitting quietly, finishing his drinks slowly. He seemed to be deep in thought, but he wouldn't talk about what he was thinking for a change. His pasty white forehead was oozing tiny drops of sweat and he seemed more reluctant than usual to drink. Perhaps he was worried, since Aldridge was actually two drinks ahead. They were nearing the twenty-drink mark.

I had a sudden flash of insight, then, into the tawdriness of the whole business. It did seem sort of tragic as I remembered the scorn of Santoni's mistress in Black River, the excessive drinking, the passing of friends with only a thin monument of paint to mark their existence, the games that meant a few dollars trading hands but not much else, and the smoke and tired music of the taverns around the state. Santoni's pale and expressionless face was the picture of someone who wanted to be somewhere else, doing something else with other people. Or, from what I now knew, with at least one other person.

I quickly ordered another beer. There was no point in brooding. Maybe he just hates losing, I decided. The hour was getting late, the contest was in full swing, and Aldridge was steadily building up a margin of confidence against his opponent. That was the idea, after all, to win this match of strength, wits, and stamina.

It turned out that Aldridge and the other man at the pool table had met several times at fishing spots around the state. He was a man who shared many of Aldridge's convictions about the right way to drink and fish. They had discussed getting together a few times, Aldridge told me later, sitting at our booth, but it had never happened.

"People aren't like fish," Aldridge explained, mysteriously. "Nice to know someone like that is out there with all the other idiots running around."

At around ten, the foursome passed our booth on their way out. They stopped to talk to Aldridge, and the younger of the two men asked about the notebook. Santoni explained about the drinking game, a bit sullenly I thought, pointedly leaving out the present tally.

"Sounds like a lot of damn foolishness," said the older man.

Aldridge laughed. "You got that right," he said.

By closing time, we had a collection of drunks who had to be herded to their cars. Those of us who were relatively sober were assigned as drivers and various complicated arrangements were made for getting the cars back to their rightful owners the next day. The gun shop men decided to sing a few rounds out there in the parking lot while the most intoxicated among us languished in the back seats. The old man actually joined them to sing "Will the Circle Be Unbroken?" He had a nice, deep singing voice and a good reason to be cheerful, since he had finally managed to defeat Santoni on a sweet drink night.

When I looked at Aldridge, it didn't seem real that so many drinks had been consumed. Where had the effect of thirty-seven double Southern Comforts gone? He was sweating, and needed to grip the edge of the car door for balance, but otherwise seemed to be having no trouble remembering the words to the song or who was supposed to drive him home.

After his own thirty-four drinks, Santoni was a mess. He sat in the passenger side of his car staring straight ahead with little comprehension while Rich pulled out into the street. His slightly curly black hair was plastered onto his forehead but stuck straight up near the crown, revealing the beginnings of a bald spot. He lurched heavily back in his seat as Rich waved and accelerated down the road toward Ann Arbor.

Ten

The system used for scoring the contest evolved with time. At first, the night's total was used to determine the winner and that person would be awarded one night or one point, though nobody had described it in just that way in the beginning. For example, on Aldridge's night to choose, if he was two drinks ahead at the end, he would be declared the winner. In order to catch up, Santoni would have to come out ahead on another night and he would be awarded a point. The total number of drinks wasn't part of the score.

One night at Andy's bar in Seney, however, the system underwent a change that probably worked to the old man's disadvantage. It was the first weekend of June and our group had been wading for brookies on the Little Two-Hearted and Sucker Rivers. Though the fishing had been great, the mosquitoes had been terrible. Luckily we had known that would be the case and we all ended up in Andy's, sitting around a couple of backgammon boards and hoping the jackass with the guitar wouldn't show up and start his plaintive and intolerable singing. Since the older locals at the bar were choosing the songs on the jukebox, the music stayed in the fifties and sixties and wasn't too loud. This seemed to please Aldridge, though he predicted that somebody would come in and start choosing hard rock or something equally annoying.

The mosquitoes and stifling heat encouraged our cynical outlook. It looked like it was going to be a weekend in which anything good would be tempered by some equally bad counter-event. The waitress said it was about time somebody drank something besides beer and whiskey, but the bartender was annoyed that we were drinking Kamikazes. Still, the waitress downed a few behind the bar to celebrate solidarity with this crowd of interesting-drinking city men from south of the Straits.

The old man played ten games of backgammon with Santoni, beating him nine times, and hardly seemed to notice that he was falling badly behind in the tally of sweet drinks. He rested while Santoni played against a young fisherman we had picked up hitchhiking on the road over from Grand Marais. The guy had just gotten a job at Colton Bay Outfitters in Ann Arbor and wanted to get down there but, for tonight, had settled on Andy's bar. Santoni was able to win three games out of five against him, and when their last game ended, the others began discussing the scoring system for the contest.

At that point in the evening Santoni was ahead thirteen drinks to nine. Since this included his customary early high speed drinking, nobody figured he would win by more than a couple of drinks. Rich was doing some figuring on a bar napkin that kept shredding under the tip of his pen.

"If this goes about the way they usually go," he began, "Bob will probably win by three, four drinks at the most. Since we started, Mr. Aldridge is ahead six nights to three."

He looked around the table to make sure we were following his set up.

"I've been looking at the drink total," he continued. "Mr. Aldridge led by one, by three, six, five, three and three on his winning nights." He pointed to the blotchy figures on the bar napkin. "Bob won by two, by three, and by five so far. That's a margin of twenty-one to ten, or eleven drinks advantage for Mr. Aldridge."

There ensued a heated discussion at this point, mostly centered on the tiny eleven drink difference after all the Herculean drinking sessions. It also seemed that Matt was making good time with the waitress. The three old men at the bar were involved in their own discussion and ignored him while he leaned across the bar whispering to the object of his new affections. However, he had been appointed to bring the next round of drinks to our table and we were therefore only partly sympathetic to his mission. After some gentle insults from our group, he finally managed to tear himself away and bring the much needed beverages. Rich continued his calculations.

"So if my prediction about tonight's outcome is more or less correct, Bob should end up only about six or seven drinks behind."

The old man glared across the table at Rich.

"So what?" he asked.

Rich gestured with the pen, which caught the middle of his notes and ripped the napkin in half.

"So," Rich said, "it's still a pretty close contest. Anyway, I think we ought to follow the total number of drinks, not the night's winner or loser, to decide the overall winner."

Santoni, who had been trying to sell everyone at the next table on the idea of a nightcrawler farm in his basement, suddenly looked over.

"What?" he said.

The proposal was explained again in simple terms for his benefit and he stared straight ahead without appearing to comprehend.

"Why?" he asked.

"Well," his brother began, "what's to keep the guy who doesn't get to choose from just quitting any time he wants to? If the total doesn't matter, there's no reason to compete."

"You mean one guy could have two drinks and the other guy could have twenty?

"Right. That wouldn't be fair. What's to keep anybody from doing that?"

"What's to keep any damn fool from doing anything he pleases?" the old man interrupted. All the heads in the group turned to look at him. "This is a drinking contest, not some lunch for accountants."

"What do you mean?" Rich asked.

"We're not a bunch of cheaters," he spat, his chin forward and a derisive expression on his face. "We come to drink and try to beat the other guy, fair and square. We don't need any new system." He was about as incensed as I'd ever seen him.

Santoni looked to be coming at least partly out of his state of confusion. He finished his drink and took another from the tray. Rich made a mark on a dry napkin.

"I don't know ..." Santoni began. Everybody now turned to look at him. "... maybe that would be better. I never thought about it that way before."

Strangely, nobody else had thought of that approach, either, though it was possible to avoid drinking entirely under the current rules. Of course that wouldn't have fit with Aldridge's way of going about things, and even Santoni seemed to love the head-to-head competition.

"We ought to change the rules that way. It's better to have a system we can count on."

The old man appealed to his opponent. "Are you going to start this two-drink nonsense now?" he asked.

Santoni shrugged his shoulders and looked pained.

"I'm just saying we ought to have some way to sort these things out. What if somebody gets it into their head to try to play it that way?"

Aldridge lost the rest of his composure and looked for a moment like the most ordinary of old, red-faced alcoholics upset by an argument with his next door neighbor. His glare followed a group of three younger men in biker jackets who had entered through the back door.

"There's only you and me, damn fool."

Santoni wouldn't meet his eyes, instead staring toward the bar where the budding romance was growing more serious. Everyone else in our group was quiet and stared into their own drinks. True to the old man's predictions, one of the newcomers walked over to the jukebox and shortly the drumbeat of hard rock began.

"Damn fools all around," Aldridge said, his face settling back into its usual dignified glower.

After a good deal more argument, it was agreed that having clearly specified rules was the better course of action. The old man, who grew even more quiet as the night continued, concentrated on getting his drinks down. He finally agreed that he would play under the new system if everyone else decided it would be better. He made up several drinks while Santoni argued his side of the issue and I wondered whether his arguments had been part of a strategy meant to buy time. At that time, I still thought he wouldn't stoop to such underhanded methods.

As it neared two a.m., the contestants sat without talking and gulped their drinks methodically, staring at one another across the table while the nausea subsided before taking up their next drinks. The old man's determination was now clearly evident. The decision that had gone against him seemed to give him new resolve, but Santoni also seemed to be drinking harder than usual to press his advantage. To the few of us who could still focus at this late hour, the tension created by this battle of wills was intense.

The jukebox had finally stopped playing. Everyone had left except for the members of our group. Matt had disappeared with the waitress. For the last hour I was the carrier of drinks, bringing them to the contestants, to Rich, to two of his buddies – one of whom slept between drinks – and to our hitchhiking adventurer, who could handle his booze surprisingly well. I took an occasional sip myself. There was an eerie quiet about the place made more stark by the steady whirr of the fan, which rotated back and forth on the corner of the bar pushing humid air around the room.

I focused on the drinking techniques of the two players. The old man, touching a glass to his lips, would suck the liquid into his mouth before swallowing it. This method, which had been the cause of our salesman's sudden exit a few sessions before, allowed him to regulate how much air he mixed with the mouthful of liquor and therefore how much of the sweet taste he had to endure. By experimenting with my own drinks I found it was possible to avoid the taste almost entirely. Unfortunately, one had to breathe sooner or later.

Santoni opened his mouth wide and poured the drinks in. He gulped them down in the same moment, which was perhaps his own method of avoiding the taste, though he claimed to enjoy the sweet drinks. I recalled that he employed the same method with whiskey. Only when the going was really tough did he allow the drinks to sit in his mouth for a brief moment before swallowing. At such moments the reluctance showed clearly on his face.

Finally, the old man dozed off. The bartender nodded to us, so we roused him and struggled to our feet. The contestants were barely in touch with the physical functions of their bodies, though each was just able to walk under his own power. I'm sure they were proud of the battle that had just ended, but neither was able to walk with anything remotely like a swagger. The final count, in a near perfect reversal of the last sweet drink session, was an incredible thirty-seven drinks for Santoni and thirty-three for his older opponent, consumed with a hamburger lunch for the young man and a grilled cheese sandwich and two bottles of Labatt's for Aldridge.

Driving the old man back to his motel in Grand Marais, I employed the time honored Upper Peninsula steering method of using the yellow line as an aiming device. It stayed more or less within view as we sped north. The cooler night air revived us both a little as it blew through the car windows. About five miles before town, he asked me to stop the car and we both got out to answer the call of nature.

"Shut it off," he said. I turned the key.

There was a moment when the dark and silence rushed in to enclose us. I remember holding the edge of the car door for balance and hearing the night sounds emerge one at a time. There was the hiss of the old man's urine as it hit the gravel, and his intermittent wheeze. The chirping of insects came up, one cricket at a time. There was the very quiet rush of wind, what little there was, through the low softwood forest near the road. Otherwise, there was very little sound.

Suddenly, a bright band of greenish light shot into the center of the sky from the north. It hung, quivering, over our heads for a moment, then swept in a wide arc to the west before disappearing. Immediately afterward, just above the horizon, there appeared a gigantic formless mass of yellow and greenish light, so bright that no stars were visible except far to the south.

"Goddamn northern lights," the old man said, nearly whispering.

It was odd to see the incredible display without any sound. After a lifetime of lightning and fireworks I expected thunder or booming sound effects to go along with anything this bright and this huge, yet in its silence the Aurora Borealis was spectacular.

Finally, the old man belched, bringing me back to the task at hand. We got back in the car. I started the engine and moved the shift lever to "drive." We sped north, the unpleasant smoke and beer smell of the tavern emanating from our clothing and settling into our noses.

As we neared the motel, I became more and more disoriented. I was barely able to steer. I vaguely remember seeing the old man holding his belly and moaning softly to himself. Too drunk and tired to focus on his problem, I pulled into the parking space outside his motel room, shifted the car into "park," and turned off the ignition. By that time, I could barely see. The old man somehow got the door open and eased himself out.

"Always come over the bridge," he said as he turned away. He swung the car door but it did not quite close. I pondered the meaning of his statement while I climbed into the back seat to pass out.

Eleven

It was during the weekend of rest after the Andy's bar session that concerns about the old man's health began to come up. The wind was gradually shifting to the north, bringing with it relief from the heavy heat of June, but the old man seemed to be sweating more than usual. His face was often tense and expressionless.

His wife came up on Saturday morning. They were originally planning to spend a week relaxing in a cabin just outside of town, but when he complained about the pains in his belly, she insisted that they drive downstate and get him to a doctor. He was not pleased and insisted that they stay over one more night. He said he wanted to sit at the bar and get a good look at Lake Superior.

That statement contained ominous undertones. Was this going to be his last visit to Grand Marais? I brooded about it while sitting with him at the Dunes Saloon. People came and went, and many greeted us, but the old man just sat with his head turned toward the windows, saying nothing to them or to me, nursing one long, two hour beer, then another.

His capacity for sitting without talking or doing anything else was much greater than mine. I grew impatient. I fidgeted with my glass, ate a bag of potato chips, and selected songs on the jukebox that I knew the old man liked. I drank a coke, a water and an orange juice. I drew naughty cartoons on the bar napkins, which I then put back into the stack by the condiment tray on the bar. I read and re-read the signs behind the bar. "You must have been born before this date in 1970." "Free beer ... tomorrow."

I felt I should stay and see to Aldridge in case he needed anything but, at the same time, the desire to do something was overwhelming. I decided to walk out to the pier. I slid my stool back and stood up. Just then Aldridge turned to me with a quarter in his hand.

"Shoot a game?" he asked. His voice was quiet and more gravelly than usual, and his face was pale.

"You okay?" I asked.

He patted his midsection with a shrug.

"Hurts."

I was relieved that he acknowledged it so openly. Maybe he would see a doctor and get an easy diagnosis like an ulcer, be ordered to quit drinking, and live another twenty years. He could fish and go to garage sales with his wife. There would be no shame in quitting the contest because of a health problem, especially since he was in the lead.

But I had a nagging suspicion that his problem would be more serious. He had been drinking heavily for at least forty years and I had long worried about him. He never seemed to get sick, but his habits were so regular and carefully organized that drinking was probably the only source of stress on his immune system. If something were to go wrong, everything might give way at once.

I racked the balls, resetting them twice because of a tiny dip in the table top at the two point dot.

"Money breaks," I said, and the old man eased himself out of his seat. He stood for a moment, gazing into space. Behind him, the front door opened and two of the members of our group came in. I nodded to them and they found a table, but Aldridge didn't seem to notice them at all. He licked his lips and turned to look at me. A lock of hair stood on end, pointing up and to his right. His eyes looked more transparent than usual and there was more tension in the skin around them, but there was the same quiet dignity in the way he held himself that there had always been.

As we played, his condition gradually deteriorated. He spoke less and less and the remaining color drained from his face. He shot a fair game even though his heart wasn't in it, but I managed an improbable bank shot on the eight and won. He seemed glad for the chance to sit down. When his wife stopped by to check on him, he asked to be taken back to their cabin.

"Call me in Ann Arbor if there's anything I can do," I said to his wife. She smiled and nodded and they went out together.

Part Two

Twelve

Back in Ann Arbor, the weather was oppressively hot during the day without the cool nights of northern Michigan to aid sleeping. I took long shifts in the cab that ended after the last of the bar traffic died down, then slept four or five hours before waking up to write in the relative cool of the morning. Writing was going badly. I was worried about the old man and it seemed irreverent to write about him when there was a possibility that he was seriously ill. Most mornings I edited the articles I had already written about the contest and tried to think of places to send them for publication.

I had spoken on the telephone with the editors of several magazines that had published my work before. When I told them about my plans for a serialized story about the drinking game, they all asked if the old man was famous. Failing that, one asked, was he dead? Interest in this sort of thing greatly increases when the subject has recently died, he said.

I called the Aldridge's home in Traverse City after a few days, but there was no answer. Santoni was at work when I called and spoke to his wife. No, they had not heard anything from the old man, either. Rich was in Ohio for some kind of conference. On the morning of the fifth day, the "S" key of my typewriter jammed. I dropped the typewriter off at Adlers, borrowed an old Impala from one of the other cabbies, and drove to Appleton Lake after buying a dozen minnows at Neff's.

The DNR had been doing fish planting experiments at Appleton for about a decade, and I had heard that there were large trout and even larger white bass living in its depths. The problem with fishing Appleton without a boat was that the bottom dropped off quickly near shore, so wading was difficult. The one sand bar that stretched out into the lake was composed of marl and clay. After trying three steps onto it I was convinced the better course of action was to fish from shore.

There were no other fishermen out, just a light breeze that pushed tiny ripples across the lake near the east shore. Huge white clouds hung in the sky, seeming close enough to touch, yet impossibly high. A few had dark bottoms that hinted at rain. The breeze whispered coolly as it moved through the trees.

I found a log to sit on and put my wadered feet in the water. I could barely detect the tugging of the minnow on my hook, straight out into the lake, under sixteen feet of water.

A slender green snake about three feet long slid through the grass toward the water's edge. When it reached the water, it moved forward smoothly and glided along the surface for a few yards, then disappeared into the grass near the stump of a sumac branch that had fallen into the water.

I watched as my line twitched, now from the minnow at the end, now from the breeze. The water kept me cool while the sun and light breeze kept the mosquitoes to a minimum. Dragonflies patrolled the air space above the lake. Occasionally a barn swallow would appear, dart out to pick up a bug, then disappear behind the trees. Far past the opposite shore, a few buzzards tilted in slow circles that I guessed were above the road. Perhaps a rabbit or opossum had been hit by a car and was lying enticingly in the ditch.

A large blue jay noticed me sitting and flew to a nearby branch to berate me. His shrill cries interrupted the serene quiet of the day. I felt I was being reprimanded for enjoying the warm laziness of the day while the old man was suffering. The bird flew closer and continued to screech. I offered a few choice words to discourage him.

When that failed, I searched around my seat to find something to throw. There was a length of wood just out of reach. I couldn't quite reach it by leaning over, so I waved my hand at the blue jay. He bobbed up and down on his perch, calling out. I transferred the fishing rod to my left hand and slid my rear end down the log toward the right side. My feet had sunk into the muck. Pulling them free one at a time, I was able to get close enough to reach the piece of wood.

I twisted my body around to get a good position for throwing. When the line tightened heavily, I at first attributed it to my own twisting motion. I cocked my arm for the throw and, suddenly, the rod bent double and was nearly pulled from my grasp. Forgetting all about the bird, I yanked back to set the hook. The bail spun, flipped open and rapped my knuckles. I flipped it back down with my free hand.

I grabbed the handle with both hands while line peeled off the reel. It sped out toward the middle of the lake. Whatever it was ran for what seemed like a full minute, easily taking a third of my line without losing any depth. It felt very strong and heavy.

At the end of the run, it made a series of short dashes back and forth with decisive tugs of its head that shook the rod as though it were tied to an Irish Setter on a leash.

The line began to spool off the reel again, this time toward the far right shore of the lake. The reel whined, then suddenly stopped. I could almost feel the fish plotting its next move. I carefully raised the rod tip. When the rod bent nearly double, the line began to zip off again, this time toward the opposite shore. Now only about a third of my line remained on the reel.

The muck made balance difficult, but I had somehow risen to a standing position. My left wrist was getting tired, so I switched the rod back to my right hand. The next run was short. At the end of it the fish began to lose some depth, still tugging solidly while rising a bit closer to the surface.

I found myself grinning and shaking out my free left hand. The hit had been too sudden and the first runs too fast to enjoy, giving me the desperate, sick feeling that the fish would break off at any moment. Now that the fight had settled into a rhythm, the adrenaline was giving me a happy buzz. I stepped back to get better footing on the shore. The fish kept tugging, not taking much more line this time.

I heard a car door slam and saw a trailer being backed into the water at the launch site across the lake. My fish made a short run, taking another ten yards of line, and the black spool showed through the short amount of monofilament that remained.

When the run stopped, I was able to get a few yards back on the spool by raising the rod, then cranking the reel while lowering it. It seemed a very strong fish for this little inland lake and felt very much alive out on the far end of the tiny line.

I began to think about the hook and the knot that held it. All the desperate mid-fight questions began to nag at me. Was my drag set light enough? Could I get away with putting this much pressure on the fish?

It would be a great story to tell the old man if I landed it, but the rush of adrenaline had turned to a knot of worry in my gut. I remembered the age of the six-pound test line, which I had not changed since the year before. I would probably lose the fish. It would break free close to shore when the strength of its desperation and the wear on the line would pair up to defeat me.

We repeated the process of gaining and losing several yards of line. The fish had yet to surface and seemed to have ample strength to run out to the end whenever it decided to do so. I wondered what kind of fish it could be. Big trout seldom jump in inland lakes, I thought, but they don't usually have this much stamina. There were several possibilities among the bass family, but the largemouth would have jumped by now, and the smallmouth, though fierce, would not have had this much stamina.

97

I noticed that the boat had been launched and was motoring silently toward me with its electric motor. Could they see that I was hooked into a fish? I hoped they would stay far enough away.

I gained line gradually as the fish made more short runs, first going deeper and moving in an arc around the pressure of the line, then trying to get more distance while rising toward the surface. It's amazing how fast the big ones learn, I thought. I was enjoying the fight again – the heavy feel of the fish, the telegraphic transfer of its strength into my hands, and the happy fatigue in my wrists and shoulders.

The boat had stopped a good distance away and the two fishermen in it sat and watched the fight. I squinted at them but from this distance couldn't make out who they were.

Finally, I caught sight of the fish. It was running near the surface and made a flash of white as it rolled over. The shade from the tree line extended out into the lake, but the fish had rolled just at the edge of it, much larger than I had imagined. I still couldn't make out what kind it was.

The boatmen edged closer. They were very courteous about the distance they kept and I began to suspect they were good fishermen.

"Want I should net it?" one called out. The voice sounded familiar.

"Naw," I said, trying to seem relaxed and professional, "I'll just beach her over here."

I was glad there was someone to witness my luck. Now there would be support for my story even if the fish broke free at the last minute. Making a gentle weaving motion underwater, it came toward shore. It looked like it could be thirty inches. A huge white bass, only the second I had ever hooked. It wasn't in my hands yet, but it looked nearly worn out. Maybe the line would hold. I pulled closer, moving my arms over my head to drag the fish close enough to grab. I could see the hook curled solidly through its upper lip.

At the sight of my hand entering the water, the fish made a sudden splash and shot back out toward the middle of the lake. I grasped the rod with both hands and held on. This was the moment when the line might go, probably at the knot where the hook had been chafing at it the whole time. My arms were tired, nearly as tired as the fish must have been. Trying to be delicate, I helped it toward shore once again.

Gradually I worked the line back onto the spool. The fish came in floating on its side, it gills working convulsively. I reached down and, grabbing its lower jaw between my thumb and forefinger, hoisted it out of the water.

"Heavy," I said.

"Buy you a beer?" said one of the men in the boat. They motored up to shore and I finally got a good look at them. It was J.P. and Matt.

"You got one?" I asked, grinning at them and lowering my arm to let the fish hang at my side, partly in the water.

"Got twenty-four cold ones."

"Damn," I said, "that was fun."

I was worn out. I set my rod in the grass and removed the hook from the fish's mouth with my free hand. It hung limp with only tiny movements of its gills. It would weigh nearly fifteen pounds.

"Too bad this is the last fish," I said.

"That's okay with us," Matt said. "We don't have any bait anyway."

I looked at them and they both burst out laughing.

We tied their hawser to the log on which I had been sitting and J.P. handed me a beer. I could hear the sound of ice in the cooler and even though the beer was only Strohs, it was very cold and delicious. I held the fish in the water with my free hand as I finished the beer.

"You have kids?" I asked Matt.

He nodded. "Yup. Wife. Two cats, mortgage. Why do you think I come out here?"

"No Barbie dolls in the woods?"

"Have another beer," he said. He took three cold ones out of the cooler and handed them around. The second seemed more bitter than the first, but it was still cold and nourishing.

"Take this fish," I said, "I can't eat it alone."

"No thanks," he said, "I don't want to clean it."

J.P. didn't want the fish either, so I lowered it fully into the water and held it upright. At first it just floated, its gills pumping and its fins working gently. I suddenly remembered the blue jay. It had vanished sometime during the fight. It must have been warning me about the bite.

After a few moments, the big white bass moved out of my hand under its own power and swam into deeper water. J.P. offered me a ride back to the boat launch, which I accepted. The mosquitoes were beginning to get more aggressive as the sun went down.

I laid my rod and bait bucket on the floor of the boat and took the middle seat. The little motor hummed and pushed us slowly across the lake. The whole west side of the water was smooth as glass, with no ripples breaking up the image of the trees on shore until the middle. Everything was animated by a spirit of gentle optimism, no doubt aided by the beers. My cheeks tingled from all the grinning I had done while battling the fish.

"What did you use," J.P. asked, "eight pound test?"

"Six pound Stren," I said examining the reel. "About forty minutes to land it, I think."

"We watched you for about half an hour."

They dropped me at the boat launch and I began to clomp toward the borrowed Impala in my waders, rod and bucket in one hand and a third beer in the other.

"Hey," J.P. called from the boat, "did you hear about Russ?"

I turned to look at him, for a moment not registering Aldridge's first name. Then I shook my head.

"They've got him over at UM hospital. Pretty bad, I guess."

Suddenly the dark color of the woods seemed ominous. I remembered the buzzards circling the dead animal in the road. I didn't want to go back into the city, but I waved to the two men in the boat, put my rod in the back seat, and started the motor. It was just dark enough to turn on the headlights.

Thirteen

The old man was sitting up in bed when I found his room. His hair was standing up on one side of his head. The hospital robe was draped in a pile of wrinkles on his belly. The shoulders that were always concealed beneath flannel shirts now poked sharply through the thin material of the robe, and his eternally sunburned skin looked even redder than usual against the white background. His face lit up for a moment when I came in, then lapsed into its usual glower.

"Heard you caught a pretty good white bass," he said, holding his thumb and forefinger about three inches apart.

"Almost seventeen pounds," I said. "How about you?"

"Nothing to goddamn do," he said. "You bring any cards?"

I had not, but there was a backgammon board on the table beside his bed. I dug it out from beneath a folded newspaper, a copy of Poor Richard's Almanac, and a book of topographical maps of Michigan lakes. We set the items at the foot of his bed. His legs formed a thin tube underneath the blanket, but otherwise there was a vast area of flat space on the bed's surface. Except where his body poked out at one end, it looked like the bedding had barely been disturbed.

He set up the board while I brought him a glass of water from the bathroom. I won the first roll with a five over his three and took the advantageous three position inside the bar. His first roll produced a four and a three.

His wife had gone home for a nap so we had the room to ourselves. There were all the usual hospital sounds, wheelchairs and stretchers being rolling past, pagers beeping, and the occasional muted, unintelligible conversation between medical students or doctors. The air in the room was dry and blew quietly out of the grates in the floor.

He pressed me for details of the fishing excursion, starting with the bait I had used and asking about the weather, the time of day and the specific spot in the lake where the fish had been hooked. We interrupted our game to locate the spot in his book of maps. It proved to be in a long, narrow arm of the deepest hole in the lake. White bass preferred the cooler water, it seemed, and fed on the edges where smaller fish might stray near. He was convinced that the lake was fed by springs, which kept it cool enough for larger trout all through the summer. The white bass, though, was bigger than any fish in Appleton Lake had a right to be.

"They're not such great eating anyway," he said, "but how was the fight?"

I told him about the long runs followed by the short, jerking forays. The fish's stamina had been remarkable, and we got into a long interview about how it had learned to resist by giving up depth instead of distance. "It did what?" he would ask, then I would explain, him moving his hand in an imitation of what the fish's motion must have been.

"No jumps?"

"No jumps. A couple of rolls near the end."

"They can goddamn learn," he said. "That's one reason I like fishing so much."

His favorite fight, from the point of view of man versus fish strategy, had been against a steelhead in the Fox River, he said. It had been a warm spring day, early enough in the season so that the bugs were not yet a problem. Since he already had two good fish, he wanted to relax, so he strolled to a small island upstream from his camp. The water was higher than usual and he had waded across to the island, using an alder branch as a cane in one hand and holding his rod in the other. The sun shone directly on the stream and, he said, he didn't have much hope of getting into anything good.

He arranged a sitting position with his feet in the water and his back against a stump. Casting across the stream into the faster water, he could feel the nightcrawler and the lead weight bumping over the rocks as they were swept downstream. The arc took them finally to the edge of the calm water below the island, where he let them sit.

"I had a couple of cold Labatt's with me," he said.

After one beer and an hour of sunshine he was nearly asleep. Then came that timeless charge of movement at the end of the line, the long loop of which straightened with each touch. After the first tug, though, nothing.

"I thought it was a sucker. Figured to pull that baby out and go back to camp."

When he set the hook, there was a moment of solid resistance, then two heavy tugs before the fish turned its body to the left and made an instant, spool squealing run fifty yards downstream. Almost out of sight beyond a curve in the river, the fish executed two classic steelhead full body leaps straight into the air, falling heavily onto its side each time. Halfway between the fish and the man there was another loud splash. A beaver, swimming upstream, had been startled by the noise and had smacked the water with its tail.

The fish, meanwhile, was darting from one side of the stream to the other, using the current to aid its resistance against the line. The old man was able to gain some line each time the fish swung into slower water, but lost nearly as much whenever it moved into the rapids.

"And I had gone up there to relax," he said. "After a couple minutes, me changing hands to shake out the tired one, that goddamned beaver showed up in the still water below the island, swimming right toward me. He came closer and closer and then, when the steelie made a fast run upstream and drifted downward to use his weight in the current, that little bastard saw me and slammed his tail on the water again.

"Now comes the amazing part. I got the fish into slower water and, because of the angle of the sun, I could see it clearly under the water. Just after the beaver surfaced for the third time, splashing again and this time getting me all wet, I could see the fish trying to tug the line down toward the bottom. There's a long patch of gravel that runs along the edge of the fast water. Each time I pulled back on the rod, that son of a bitch stuck his nose in the gravel and dug in. Between his weight, the current, and the resistance of the gravel, I couldn't move him at all.

"Well, this went on for a long time. He was getting a good rest that way, and every now and then he tried to make a break into the fast water, but he always ended up back there with his nose in the rocks. Damnedest thing. Never saw a fish do that before or since."

I had won two games while he narrated this story and we paused while he sat back to catch his breath. I paged through the Almanac to see if there was going to be any good fishing in the next week. The old man used the remote to turn on the television. Poor Richard said the barometer would rise all week, making for great outdoor activities but adding to the farmer's water troubles, as usual. Channel four remained divided about Turkey's latest threat to occupy the much weakened Iraq that would result from a war with the West.

"Ought to blow up the whole lot of 'em," Aldridge said, shutting off the TV and tossing the control on the foot of bed.

"And what finally happened with the steelhead?" I asked.

"Almost cut the damn line," he said. "My wrists and forearms were so tired I could barely hang on to the rod. When he wedged his nose in the gravel the final time, I just took all the slack out of the line to hold him, waded over there and reached down to scoop him up by the gills. His nose was worn raw by the gravel trick.

"My fishing buddies had already gone back downstate, so I had this twelve pound fish to eat by myself. I filleted that bastard and made a fish boil with onions and potatoes in a big pot over the fire. Ate almost half that night and had some cold the next morning with toast and coffee. A bear finished off what was left with the potatoes and onions the next night when I forgot to put the pot in the trunk. Smart fish. Delicious, too."

When I was there, the old man hadn't eaten in twenty-four hours. He was scheduled to go in for abdominal surgery the next morning.

Fourteen

Soon after returning home from my visit with Aldridge, I got a call from Linda, a former college girlfriend. She and I had enjoyed debating the merits of various writers in our college days, but we had been out of touch for five years. She had gotten married, she said, and was in town with her new husband. Why didn't we get together for a drink?

They opted for an elegant restaurant in Ann Arbor called the Earle that I didn't love, but I agreed to go since it would only be for an hour or two. A friend of mine named Donny Prior played piano there and I thought, if nothing else, it would be a chance to say hello to him.

My shift started at eleven, so I decided to walk over to the dispatch office and pick up a cab before going to the Earle. We had entered the first week of a weather pattern that brought rain for a couple of days, then followed it with three days of clear skies before starting to rain again. The air, recently cleansed, was soft and lucid, though a bit too warm, and walking through town near sunset was a real pleasure. Everything shone with a quiet radiance.

One of the big old elm trees that had survived the blight towered over my head. Each leaf had a precise clarity when I looked directly at it, but the outline of the tree itself was soft and shimmered with the movement of all the leaves in the breeze. I stared at it with unfocused eyes while a cardinal, illuminated by the setting sun, called out from a branch near the top.

At the office, I picked up the keys to my cab. The dispatcher mentioned that the police had been cracking down on us for speeding and rolling through stop signs, so I should be extra careful. I thanked her and went out to the parking lot to find the vehicle. The inside of the cab was musty and synthetic, in sharp contrast to the clean beauty of the weather, but the solid familiarity of the seats, mirrors, knobs and dials was comforting. I was temporarily fond of the simplicity of my life.

I drove back into town. There was a parking space open just around the corner from the restaurant.

When I walked in, the actual piano I had hoped to hear was closed and silent. Instead, not unhappily, a recording of a Tchaikovsky concerto was playing on the stereo. Candles burned at every table and the brass railing in front of the bar glowed with their rich golden reflections. The racks behind the bar were lined with expensive liqueurs. Over equally pricey dinners, the clientele spoke to one another in quiet tones, but somehow the atmosphere didn't ring true for me. The restaurant was located in the basement, for one thing, and smelled of mildew, and the hostess had worked in virtually every restaurant in town. I had known her casually for years. She had dated a friend of mine and had hurt his feelings badly when they broke up.

My friend Linda and her husband hadn't shown up yet, so I sat at the bar and ordered a Heineken. The bartender brought me the beer in a tall, conical glass, which nicely highlighted the flavor of the beer. On the other hand, in spite of his pressed white shirt and narrow black tie, he smelled strongly of yesterday's perspiration.

I thought about Aldridge's matter-of-fact approach to drinking and to life and wondered what he was going through at that moment. Would he be able to sleep the night before his surgery? Was he fretting over the lack of food? Was fear of the knife keeping him awake? I could picture him sitting up in bed, illuminated by the moonlight, sipping water and thinking back to his fishing adventures between moments of worry. I didn't know whether his wife would be with him, but I doubted she would be allowed to stay through the night.

Though he was alone much of the time, it was usually in places where other people came and went, places with natural or human noises, smells, and the grit that life drops as it passes by. The clean loneliness of the hospital wouldn't appeal to him at all, since it couldn't hear his stories or accommodate itself to his outdated way of thinking. I thought of calling him, but decided it would be insulting to suppose that he needed propping up.

My friend arrived with her new husband. When I saw his childish, pock-marked face, I realized that I had met him two or three times before. After each time, I forgot his name, and here he was married to someone who had been my girlfriend in college. His handshake was limp and clammy.

They had just come from dinner. He had been drinking red wine, it seemed, and was prepared to hold forth at length on several topics of his choosing. We found a table and he ostentatiously scanned the list of brandies and cognacs, his finger darting to the price column to help him decide which drink was best. He selected the second most expensive cognac, pronouncing its French name perfectly to the waitress and telling his new wife what she should order. To my surprise, she obeyed meekly. To punish myself for getting into this situation, I ordered Benedictine. I was feeling congested and the monkish liqueur tasted and smelled exactly like cough syrup.

Linda and I compared notes on a few old classmates, frequently interrupted by her spouse's comments on the person in question. It was hard to understand how she had gotten involved with this fellow, who was the personification of every trait we had disliked about academics. However, when he began to hold forth on the implicit social challenges of the Twentieth Century liberal arts approach to literature, she gave me an amused look. Indeed, it wasn't difficult to get him started on a lecture about almost any subject. He would announce his view, ask for a comment that he would promptly interrupt or correct, then pontificate until the topic was suitably exhausted. Even the people at the nearby tables, who had looked annoyed at his podium voice, were smiling. Well, I thought, she has got herself a court jester.

His face became deeply red as the evening progressed. Each glass of cognac increased the shininess of his complexion.

I began to long for the bitter taste of beer and the quiet, regulated pace of an evening of drinking with the old man. Besides his dignity and penchant for long periods of silence, when Aldridge did talk, his words were usually the well considered opinions of someone who had lived a long, full life. His views came from a wide base of experience and his comments reflected an outlook developed by living his particular sort of life. His was a reality of working, fishing and drinking, rather than haughty academic theories upheld by argumentative wind-baggery.

Aldridge had no special desire to impress. He seemed neither over confident nor especially concerned with what people thought of him. It would have been unlike him to battle for position in the social hierarchy, at least by the time I knew him.

With this thought, I wondered for a moment why he had agreed to the drinking match in the first place. He had always enjoyed winning a game of eight-ball, of course, but I thought his intention was to add enjoyment to time spent drinking and conversing. I never thought of him as an especially competitive person, or a blowhard. His great character weakness was the inability to suffer fools, which suggested that he had taken up the match in a moment of pique over his younger opponent's rash challenge, but it did not immediately explain why he continued the match with such seriousness.

As I listened to our distinguished professor hold forth on how to get one's fiction published, he having never done so but still full of the most widely respected academic doctrine, I wondered what it would take to shut him up. Were all the universities filled with such claptrap? I hadn't known my professors well enough to know if they were as disconnected from reality as this refined gentleman but, if they were, it was no wonder my education had done so little to help me get a job. That was my excuse at the time, at least.

Finally it was time for me to get to work. There was a last moment of awkwardness when we paid the bill. I had calculated the tip and left it on the table, but the professor decided to use his credit card. He was short on cash, so he added the amount of my tip to the total amount he charged and took the bills I had contributed. He counted them. Perhaps the twenty percent I left did not accord with the peer reviewed socio-economic analysis of Ivy League experts. He looked at me with icy condescension, but by that time I had stopped caring about his opinions and I let it pass.

In the un-literary real world outside, the rainy part of the weather cycle had returned with a vengeance. We stood under the awning at the doorway, watching sheets of water fall.

"Well," said Linda, "I'm not going out into this."

To my surprise, her husband meekly volunteered to bring the car around. He actually headed out into the rain without immediately melting. In a sheepish tone his wife said, "I keep him around for moments like this."

Which restored her to my good graces.

When the car pulled up, we bid each other goodnight. She got in, they drove off, and I got set to make my own way through the rain.

Fifteen

I spent the rest of June driving as many hours as I could, fishing occasionally with little success, and hiding out from the heat in the afternoons by shooting nine-ball at the Eight-Ball Saloon. I got to be good friends with John Spears, one of the bartenders, who would give me my first beer free. He wasn't an avid fisherman, but wanted to get more into the sport, so we often talked about arranging a time to borrow a boat and try our luck.

On an evening early in July, I was sitting across the bar from him discussing variations in types of hangovers when the salesman friend of Santoni's named Ken showed up with three of his friends. I saw the reflection of his trademark baseball cap in the mirror behind the bar. When you looked at the hat while it was on his head, the writing on the front was gibberish, but if you turned your head sideways, or if he took the hat off and tipped it to the side, the words resolved themselves into a warm greeting reading, "Go Fuck Yourself." I continued the conversation without turning my head.

118

They piled in noisily, scanning the empty room for someone to recognize their existence. Ken was the first to succeed. He strutted up to me and put his hand on my shoulder while he ordered drinks. We were good friends, it seemed. I should come over and sit with them, he said, play a couple games of eight-ball. I couldn't think up an excuse quickly enough so I agreed to go over after I got my next beer. He went to sit at the table chosen by his companions.

Spears threw me an accusatory look. I shook my head.

"He shoot a good game?" he asked.

"How could he?" I said. "Just look at his clothes."

He opened a bottle of Labatt's and set it in front of me on the bar.

"Here's your imported beer, sir."

"Drop dead," I suggested.

We had agreed that hangovers were located mainly in the stomach and the head, but that sometimes they would manifest in very specific locations such as the sinuses or the throat. I thought back on my travels for the drinking contest and told him about one morning after a session when the contestants and several of the followers had spent the night at the old man's house in Ann Arbor.

The drinking had been done at Big Daddy's Bar in Saline, and I had ended up with the responsibility of driving half the crew back to town. It had been a boisterous evening until we walked over the threshold of the Aldridge home, at which point everybody fell silent in deference to the lady of the house.

They had all fallen asleep quickly, Rich and a couple of his buddies from Bridgewater in the guest bedroom and Santoni and I on a couple of couches in the living room. The next morning, I awoke to the sound of voices in the kitchen.

The two contestants had been the first to rise, though even the combined drink total of all the rest of us barely equaled the number consumed by either one of them. I had expected to be the first one up since I didn't sleep well in strange houses, but there they were, Aldridge standing at the stove watching a pot of coffee, and Santoni sitting at the kitchen table. They nodded to me as I came in. Aldridge was explaining his method for brewing coffee, which was to add grounds to a pot of cold water, place it over high heat, and watch it until it boiled. Just at the boiling point, he would shut off the burner and let the pot sit for four or five minutes until it was brewed and nearly cool enough to drink. Santoni, who said that he never used anything but an automatic drip coffee maker, seemed fascinated by the old man's system and kept nodding attentively.

There was something odd about his fascination, however, and I watched him for a few minutes to see if I could figure out what it was. He stared directly at Aldridge while listening, which was unusual since he usually didn't meet the old man's eyes. Also, his own eyes were a bit too wide and, instead of moving them to follow the old man, he turned his whole head, owl-like.

The old man spoke in a low voice and described in great detail the reasons for his system. He said something about the oils in the coffee being released by the heat and that the trick was to get just the right amount of flavorful oils out of the beans without getting the bitterness. He droned on in his low, teacherly voice. After a few more minutes of watching the two men interact with one another, I realized that they were both still drunk.

"What did you do when you first got up?" I asked Santoni.

"Took a leak," he said. "Then took four aspirin with a glass of water and had some orange juice. I wanted a Coke but they don't have any here."

"And you, sir?" I asked Aldridge.

"Bout the same thing," said the old man, "minus the dreaded Coke."

121

"What time do you usually sober up?" I asked them.

The old man grinned. He said he felt fine but that he wouldn't be completely sober until he awoke from his afternoon nap. Santoni, staring straight ahead at the coffee grounds boiling over the edge of the pot, stated that he would be sober by noon. He said he sometimes went to work with a morning-after drunk but, even though he could do his job well enough, the customers didn't like it because his breath smelled of booze. By lunchtime, he said, he could meet with his boss with impunity because his fast metabolism had totally burned up the alcohol.

It seems they had both worked out systems to reduce the severity of the hangovers that would have otherwise come in the middle of the day, but each betrayed his intoxicated state in characteristic ways. Santoni had his staring and, looking more closely, I saw that he was sweating heavily as he always did late in drinking sessions. He also did, in fact, give off the strong, sweet odor of a drinker. The old man's hands shook more than usual and he held his coffee cup in both hands to drink. He blew his nose every five minutes or so but, besides that, his reserve masked any other symptoms.

After we nursed our coffee for half an hour, Mrs. Aldridge came down and began to prepare breakfast. When the wonderful aromas rose to the second floor, the remaining sluggards stirred themselves and appeared, looking much worse for wear than the two contestants. They complained of various hangover symptoms and were treated with the aspirin, water and orange juice method. The key difference between them and the two combatants was that, while they had drunk enough to have been intoxicated the night before, they were already sober. They would feel bad enough to stay away from the stuff for a day or two while Santoni and Aldridge could easily pick up where they had left off the evening before.

Spears remarked that there were a few men who came into the bar every day in the early afternoon and who often drank until closing time. They would do this day in and day out and had been doing it as long as he had been tending bar there. There was no way, he reasoned, they could sober up completely in the short interval between one day and next. Such men, he figured, never had to deal with hangovers, either.

I wanted to continue the discussion with him, but the party of salesmen was starting to call out, wondering when I was going to join them. I shrugged fatalistically, stood up, and walked over to the table.

Ken was describing a big washer and dryer sale he had made that day and his friends were listening intently. They all laughed when he revealed his commission.

"And they thought they were getting a great deal!" he cackled.

After a few minutes, it was clear that he was a sort of ringleader to this group of small time scam artists. In the company of Aldridge and Santoni he played only a supporting role, not much more than an occasional partner for a game of eight-ball or backgammon and the butt of a joke now and then. Here, he was cocky and in command.

"Should we play a game?" one of the others asked. He waved his hand in permission and the meek fellow went to rack the balls. The break had to be performed twice since his first effort missed the balls entirely.

Inspired by my visit to the table, Ken began to tell the story of the drinking contest, constructing for himself a role as instigator, rule maker, and objective observer of events. His friends played pool badly as they listened. He described me as an assistant, part time driver, and heir to Aldridge's outdated traditions. Each time I tried to suggest an alternative version of events he would counter by saying, "That's your opinion."

In his view, Santoni was a young, noble hero, fighting for more liberal drinking customs and a place in regional history. That there had to be an impressive champion of tradition in order for the contest to be worthy of attention escaped him entirely. He saw Aldridge as a useless old alcoholic nearing the end of his life

124

who was often unreasonable and bitter. The implication, which would probably have been stated outright had I not been present, was that he was only leading because of his temperamental manipulation of the dates and locations of the sessions. Those of us in his camp were supposedly there reluctantly, waiting for the first sign of weakness to defect to Santoni's band. I could hardly believe my ears.

I was formulating a plan of escape, intending to leave as quickly as possible, but Spears suddenly appeared at the table with a new round of drinks.

"We didn't order these yet," Ken objected.

"Courtesy of your host," said my friend.

"I have to take off," he said to me with a conspiratorial smile. "See you later."

I was left with the sales crew, which was hearing about how Santoni's support group consisted of a famous water skier, a gorgeous camp counselor from Acme and several senior salespeople from among the heroes of this group. Ken told them I shot a pretty good game of eight-ball and they pressed me to play. One of the cronies flashed out a fancy lighter to light the boss's cigarette.

Some indignities are too much to bear. The old man was sixty-seven years old and had fought in World War II. He had lived a rewarding life and was happily married. Santoni, though improving with age and experience, was a thirty-two year old loudmouth whose noisy, childish friends made their bread by conning housewives into buying overpriced appliances. He was running around with a grown up girl scout while his wife and kids sat at home waiting for him. Moreover, Aldridge was lying in a hospital bed recovering from a serious operation. Where I came from, you didn't talk badly about people who were ill. I told this to Ken while one of his friends shoved a pool cue in my hand.

"You'll see," he said, misunderstanding me, "from now on Bob is going to start winning. Your old man doesn't stand a chance."

I was fed up with his inability to grasp the foolishness of what he was saying. I stood stiffly in front of him, the pool cue forgotten in my right hand.

"What's your stake in it?" I asked. My voice sounded odd. "You're not the one doing the drinking."

I knew I was going to hit him, whatever he said.

"Don't get worked up, kid," he drawled. "Everybody has to lose sometime."

It was unsatisfying even as I did it. Instead of the sharp crack I had been hoping for, followed by the sudden drop of his body, the contact between my fist and the side of his head was a dull thud. He just stood there vacantly, looking at me in disbelief. His friends were frozen in place, awaiting some instructions on how to behave.

I remember hearing Jim Morrison on the jukebox singing "People are strange, when you're a stranger. Faces look ugly when you're alone." It occurred to me in the moment that, despite the appropriateness of the words, the song was far too old for the day and age, forgetting that in the evenings the bar was a refuge for aging hippies and Vietnam veterans.

I wanted him to come at me, though I realized he would never understand why I was fighting him. Certain idiocies should be punished with physical pain, I reasoned, just for their existence. The replacement bartender came around the bar to intervene but, before he could approach, Ken sat down heavily. He was out of breath and beads of sweat had appeared on his face.

"You little shit," he said. Tears sprang to his eyes. The overweight, reddened face was truly unpleasant, glaring at me while droplets coursed down his cheeks. Someone took the pool cue from me. My knuckles hurt.

"You better be going," the bartender said.

I started meekly for the door. The last thing I saw inside the bar was Ken's group of loyal friends gathered around him in a tight group.

"Truth and justice suffer another stupid defeat," I told a parking meter as I walked back to my apartment. The parking meter made no reply. I wasn't sure whether the defeat had come despite my efforts or because of them. At the time I still thought people could be persuaded to change their opinions with reason and thoughtful discussion. However righteous I may have felt, of course, I hadn't tried either of those methods.

Sixteen

After his stay in the hospital, Aldridge refused to consider forfeiting the match. He insisted on beginning again as soon as they could arrange a mutually convenient time, and even suggested that the rules be changed to make the sessions more strenuous than they had been. He said he wanted them to continue drinking over two, three, or even four days, so that the drink total for the entire weekend or period of days would be considered to decide the winner of that session. The total number of drinks would go toward his total. Santoni insisted that it was too late to make such a drastic change.

Aldridge and his wife went to stay at their cabin near Traverse City while the problem was worked out. Rich spent an hour on the phone each day, trying to get the parties to agree to play by the old rules. This was the hottest part of the summer and most of us were hoping the game wouldn't continue. We were worn out from traveling and drinking too much, even with the six week hiatus.

Finally, Santoni contacted me and asked if I would talk with Aldridge about continuing the contest. He said Aldridge respected me more than the others, which I was surprised to hear, but I was happy to have an excuse to go to Traverse City. I called Aldridge's wife and made arrangements to stay with them for a few days. She agreed to pick me up at the bus station.

The old man was a little pale but otherwise looked well rested and fairly healthy. He ate well the first night I was there and we all went to bed early. The next morning we decided to take the boat out and go trolling on Cedar Lake.

In his little boat he was relaxed and talkative. We started around the west shore of the lake with three rods out. The surface of the water was quiet, reflecting the clear sky, except in the long disturbance of the wake, which tailed out behind us. He pointed out a blue heron wading near shore. The huge bird moved smoothly along, its head swaying forward and back, then froze as we passed. The soft hum of the electric trolling motor began to lull me to sleep. I dragged one hand in the water while the old man told a story about fishing for smallmouth bass in West Bay.

I was barely listening, but I remember the old man's stiff back framed against the forest and the sky, how it must have been a repeat of a thousand other rides around this or some other lake in the quiet mornings of his life. Like the heron, he blended in with his surroundings, almost invisible until he moved. He was part of the natural landscape, and I've never lost that image of his silhouette against the tree line.

We were halfway around the lake. Just about the time I would have fallen fully asleep, there was a great tug on one of the lines. The old man grabbed the rod and heaved back on it to set the hook. Line began tearing off the reel, spinning the spool with a high-pitched squeal. He was onto something big.

I cut the speed of the motor and turned the boat around to follow the fish. The rod stayed bent nearly double, but at least our progress stopped the line from peeling off.

I reeled in the other two lines and guided the boat. Aldridge continued to sit stiffly, holding the taut rod with both hands with no expression on his face. I wanted him to show some excitement or give me the rod, but he just held on and waited for the fish to tire. The three of us were working our way toward shore.

About thirty yards from us, a great brown shape rose to the surface and shot into the air, its head shaking. On the second jump, the silver lure in its mouth glinted brightly and separated from the fish, sailing toward us in a long arc through the air. At the end of its flight, it plopped into the water next to the boat.

The old man continued to sit as he reeled in the slack line. His composure was amazing.

"Big goddamn muskie," he said. "Thought they were gone out of this lake."

We laid the rods along the inside of the boat and drifted. The air had warmed up as the sun rose and Aldridge opened a beer. I noticed that his hands were shaking. Now that he had fought and lost the big fish, he seemed frail and tired.

"Let's go in," he said. "Too hot to fish anymore."

Later, we sat on his back porch and watched the birds coming to the feeder. We discussed the future of the drinking contest. He had taken a nap and was happily cranky, criticizing all my suggestions but enjoying his role as the cantankerous old S.O.B. He spat out into the yard. I had never seen him so relaxed.

"Let's let Santoni stew for a while," he said. "It won't hurt him much."

I was surprised and told him so.

"I thought you were above using such psychological tricks," I said.

He spat again.

"I'm above nothing. Did you ever try drinking twenty-three Kamikazes in one sitting?"

A blue jay landed heavily on the edge of the feeder, scaring all the songbirds into the bushes.

Seventeen

Aldridge's wife had spent some time teaching in junior high schools but, during the last fifteen years of her career, she taught in the fifth and sixth grades. As nice as she was, she still retained some of the exaggerated diction of the elementary school teacher. Any point she made was clear to us grown-ups long before she finished explaining it. Aldridge seemed to ignore her speech patterns, but many of the drinkers who followed the contest made no secret of the fact that they preferred his company when he was alone. I found her pleasant in spite of her tendency to over explain, and since I wanted to learn as much as possible about the old man, I spent time around her rather often.

In this way I learned of his respect for me, which others had mentioned but which I had had trouble accepting. She and I had eaten lunch together at a nearby diner while the old man took his nap. I finished my fried egg sandwich and drank coffee while she picked at a salad. Between bites of lettuce and cucumber, she brought up the subject.

"I don't know if I ever thanked you properly for what you did while Russell was in the hospital."

I had copied my attempts at documenting the contest and had given them to Aldridge during one of my visits.

"He enjoys those stories so much. I remember him talking to one of the doctors about them. It was in the evening before his surgery, you know. He was grouchy because they wouldn't let him eat, and the doctor was explaining the operation to him. It was Doctor Sandweiss, I think. He was so helpful, you know.

"Russell listened to what he had to say, everything they were going to do to him. He hates hearing about it. He won't talk about his chemicals at all, he just takes them without saying anything. You know, he's not supposed to drink at all anymore."

She was making me feel her frustration and worry, which I wanted no part of. She was angry and scared, but of course there was nothing either of us could do besides wait and let the treatment take its course. I tried to change the subject.

"So he liked the articles?"

She stirred her tea and gave herself a moment to calm down. After a moment, she smiled.

"He's like a child with them. He loves reading about himself. After Doctor Sandweiss finished explaining the procedure, Russell told him about the stories. Can you imagine?

"Do you know what he said? He said they should be careful not to damage anything while they were in there. Take out the cancer, but leave everything else alone. He said he spent over sixty years getting everything in shape and not to mess it up."

Her emotions were getting the best of her. She wanted to laugh at her husband's childishness, but the threat of his illness was making her desperate as she recounted his words. Her eyes were red and shiny with latent tears.

"He said he wanted to finish up the contest so the story could be completed. Doctor Sandweiss scolded him and told him that drinking was out of the question. Russell said he understood, but of course he doesn't. The doctor went out and Russell glared at me. He just glared."

She sighed again. "He was really angry. He said the doctor lacked humanity. He said he didn't understand what was really important in life. Can you imagine? I think he was mad because the doctor didn't ask to see the stories."

It was funny to imagine the old man in a snit because someone didn't want to read about him. Still, I could sympathize with his frustration, and my vanity was a little piqued. I was getting tired of hearing my articles referred to as "stories," but there didn't seem to be any point in upsetting her further by insisting that she identify them correctly. And in a way I viewed the description as a kind of promotion from journalist to writer and I thought I'd let that stand, at least with her. Before that, it hadn't occurred to me to write fiction.

"Anyway," she went on, "he said later you were the only person he knew who would amount to anything. He thinks you understand him."

The full force of the old man's admiration was a bit too much for me. I was embarrassed, so I ordered a slice of apple pie to stay busy. I stared at my plate while I ate it and thought about the differences between women and men. I was used to the company of men and their oblique ways of expressing friendship. Aldridge himself had never told me what his wife just had. He had barely mentioned the articles at all.

At the time I thought I preferred a man's sort of friendship. It seemed much neater to have a beer or shoot a game of pool. On the other hand, if she hadn't told me the story, I never would have known how much he liked my gift. Afterward, we went back to the house to see if he needed anything when he awoke.

Eighteen

Shooting eight-ball with the old man the next day, I
remembered the conversation with his wife and tried to put the
emotions together with the face and body before me. He was
equipped with few means of emotional expression. Watching him
walk from the bar to the pool table, as he prepared himself for a
shot, I realized how his body had become specialized for drinking.

His arms and legs were dissipated from lack of exercise.
Though he looked reasonable in his flannel shirts and work pants,
when I looked closely I could see the sharp angularity of his
shoulders and see that the bulk of his arms and legs was supplied
by the heavy fabric and not by the limbs themselves. His pool
game was good, great even, but the quality of his break came from
dexterity rather than strength.

Supported on his spindly legs was his belly. This was the
vessel where his body stored the vast quantities of drink. It wasn't
enormous, nor did it hang down as it does on men who are

138

otherwise heavy. There was simply a wide round space on the front of his body that was the axis for all his movement. After sliding off the barstool, he set his feet carefully on the floor and moved smoothly across to the pool table. When he shot, the belly provided what impetus there was to drive the cue. On shots for which he had to reach, he pressed it against the table for stability. It didn't seem to have been altered much by the surgery.

Welling up from this source of movement were his small chest and his reddened neck and head. I could only imagine him with his shirt off, but I supposed that there was a sharp line at the base of his neck where the sunburn stopped. Above that line the skin was supported by the bones of the skull, but it was bronzed and wrinkled.

The mouth was used to take in alcohol and to utter cynical remarks or tell fishing stories. It was dry and controlled in repose but, when the old man spoke, you could see moisture and the angry red color inside. The eyes expressed seriousness or cynicism. Inside the head there were calculations, daydreams, fishing stories, and occasional headaches in the days after drinking. The liver had replaced the heart as the organ of major importance. At first, I couldn't see any room for the softer kinds of emotions his wife had described to me.

But as I sat and watched him shoot, I thought I could feel a kind of fatherly warmth in his personality. I couldn't locate exactly where it came from but, when he sank the thirteen ball with a clever bank shot, he looked over at me and winked. Later, I heard him humming along with the jukebox. We had vegetable soup with his wife when she came to pick him up, and he ate a few of the chips I had ordered with my hamburger.

All this careful watching had made me sensitive to details. Every casual gesture started to seem like an indication of the gentler old man inside. When he told a story about ice fishing on Saginaw Bay as a child, I could see how he used his fishing tales to keep people around him. It was strange to be listening and be part of the conversation while at the same time keeping myself separated as an observer.

Perhaps those gestures had been there all along. Certainly it would never have occurred to me to look for them before my conversation with his wife.

He soon grew tired and she insisted they go back to their place. I watched as they went out together, he leaning on her arm and walking stiff legged, moving his belly along and looking about the same on the outside as any other weary old man.

I stayed at the bar and practiced my bank shots. Matt was going to be at the next drinking session and I wanted to continue to be an important factor in his losing streak.

Part Three

Nineteen

The old man finally agreed to resume the contest under the old rules. In an attempt to keep the drinking in a favorable realm, for the next session he selected a tavern in Clare with almost no discernable character other than the moderately tasty broasted chicken it served. It was in a plain white rectangular building. Even the name was forgettable. There was no shortage of parking spaces in front, nor of small town suspicion inside. Though a couple of the patrons there knew Aldridge, they looked at the rest of us critically.

There was not even any music playing on the jukebox when we went in. There was just the stale quiet of the early afternoon and the idle pool table, which stood like a barrier between us and the two unplugged pinball machines at the back of the room.

"Michelob on tap?" the old man asked, after making slow progress onto a barstool. The bartender answered with a nod.

"Jim Beam with Michelob chasers," Aldridge said to Santoni, who shrugged and sat down next to him at the counter.

Rich, Matt and I went to sit at the table nearest the pool table. It was just underneath the television, which was also unplugged. Our table ordered light drinks, mostly beer, and various lunches, but the two contestants sat close and talked to one another in quiet voices while the grouchy bartender glared at them from the other side of the counter. I couldn't hear what they were discussing.

Rich had brought a cribbage board and began to beat Matt and me in a steady succession of games. I couldn't understand how he could make such consistent fools of us in a game that depended so much on luck, so I asked him to play the old man. Rich took the board over and sat at the counter to play. Aldridge won the first deal.

During the game there was a great bluster at the front door and Big Jon pushed through the opening, followed by his big family. There were five of them including Jon's brother, wife, and two sons. Jon's wife was the smallest of them at five feet ten inches tall, and the rest of us who stood up to be introduced felt like small children. His twin sons, who at thirteen must have weighed five hundred pounds between them without being particularly overweight, were very shy and went to play pool as soon as they had ordered Cokes.

We pushed the two tables together and everybody found a seat except the old man and Rich. They were finishing their game at the counter. The old man was already on third street while Rich had barely rounded the first corner. When Santoni had found a chair and had gotten a fresh round in front of him, Jon began to tell us a story about Olaf, the singing Swede.

"I know this one," Aldridge said over his shoulder.

It seems that Jon and his brothers had been trolling for lake trout at a certain spot in Lake Superior and decided to change tactics and anchor near a breakwater to cast for pike. They anchored on the leeward side of the breakwater within shouting distance of another boat with four men in it.

'That's where I met Russell," he said. I had never heard Jon talk so much. "He and these other guys are casting for northerns, same as us. They had been there since early morning.

"'Got some fish?' they shout at us and we shout back, 'No!' 'We got some, yah,' they say, and one of the guys uses both hands to lift up a metal hook stringer with five northerns on it. The smallest one is ten pounds, at least. They all thought that was pretty funny.

"So we fish there alongside them for about an hour with nobody catching anything in either boat. We're quiet as hell, casting our arms off, trying to see what kind of lures they're using and lifting up our anchor now and then to drift closer to their boat. Still, no fish."

The old man had won the cribbage game, proving nothing about luck but showing once again that he was better than everybody else at just about everything, and he and Rich came over to take seats at the table. I noticed that he moved very slowly off his stool at the counter, but I didn't worry since the expression on his face was relaxed and his color was good.

Jon took a long drink of his Michelob. He scratched his head.

"They catch on to us after a while. They look over and see us moving closer and closer, and still no fish, and pretty soon one of 'em smiles at us and says ..."

"You guys hungry?" Aldridge finished his sentence for him. "That was Cousin Emil."

"Your cousin?" Rich asked.

"No, I'm not Swedish. Everybody calls him Cousin Emil."

Jon continued. "'I weigh two-hundred-ninety pounds,' I say, 'I'm always hungry.' So they say 'c'mon over!'

"We pull up alongside their boat and tie up there. The greatest smells are coming out of that boat. 'What you got?' I ask, and they say, 'Swedish meatballs, what else? And boiled lake trout, Elkie's homemade bread. And what's in that bowl? Potato salad."

The old man shook his head, remembering the extraordinary meal.

"Dad," one of Jon's sons complained, "You're making us hungry."

The two giant boys held their bellies. Their faces looked like they could have gobbled up all of us and still had room for dessert.

"Order some lunch, then," Jon told them. They turned to their mother and began to discuss what they should eat.

"We sit there and eat that lunch and drink a ton of beer and just have the greatest time. Nobody even thinks about fishing for about two hours."

Santoni signaled for more drinks and made a note in the scoring booklet.

"Finally we untie the boats. After joking around and planning to meet for the all-you-can-eat perch dinner at the Elks Lodge the next Friday, we go back to fishing. I get so I can't stand it anymore and I say across to the other boat, 'How the heck did you catch all those northerns?'

"Russell and those Swedes start laughing again and they must of laughed for about ten minutes. When Emil recovers enough to talk he points to one of the other guys, a quiet guy who I don't think said even one word while we were tied up to them, and says, 'This is Olaf, the singing Swede.'

"'So?' I say, 'I don't get it.'

"'Whenever Olaf sings, the fish start biting.' These guys are grinning from ear to ear and look over at my brothers ...'"

Jon looked over at his brother, who nodded to confirm the story. Both the brother and the old man were grinning as the story continued.

"... and they go, 'Yeah, right.'

"And Emil just smiles and is casting away, and pretty soon Olaf starts to sing this song in Swedish."

"It was the worst singing I ever heard," Jon's brother said.

"But before you know it, Emil and Russ are both into big fish, and not long after that I hook into something that pulls like hell. We couldn't believe it."

I reached over and picked up the record book. Ordinarily by this time the contestants would have been well into the high teens, but they were running even at nine drinks apiece, which meant that Santoni had not had his early run of fast drinks, nor was Aldridge showing any special advantage of drinking on a whiskey night. I watched them for a moment and saw that both were just sipping at their drinks.

"So I land this twenty pounder," Jon continued, "and the Swedes start to get their fish near the boat ..."

"That was about the size of that white bass you got out of Appleton wasn't it?" Aldridge interrupted to say to me.

I nodded. "Just about."

"You got a twenty pound white bass?" Jon's brother asked. "Jesus. I never saw one that size."

"Fought like hell," I said.

Jon's sons had inhaled their lunches and more cokes and went to ask the bartender to plug in the pinball machines. We all watched with delight while the two gigantic kids sweated in fear of this tiny, shriveled up old bartender. With no excess of good cheer he came out from behind the bar to start the machines. The boys stood close together wringing their hands and waiting for the machines to light up.

Our delight turned to cowardice when the bartender came over to collect empty glasses. He wiped the table quickly and pushed a puddle of condensation from a beer glass into Rich's lap. Rich immediately apologized. Somehow the bartender managed to convict all of us with his facial expression while at the same time performing a sort of bow of respect in front of the old man.

"Thanks, Eddy," Aldridge said as the man walked away. The table was silent for a moment. We sat uncomfortably, listening to the bells chiming from the games in front of the two boys.

"Well," Jon started again, "Russ gets his fish near the boat and it turns out to be one of those big eely things, what do they call them?

"Lawyers," said Aldridge.

"It's huge, but of course nobody wants it in the boat so the fourth guy, Eino, reaches down with the pliers and pulls out the hook.

"Emil finally brings his own fish to the side of the boat and it's a really big northern. I mean really big. That thing must have gone four feet or more and we're going bananas over in our boat while Eino looks down at the fish, still in the water.

"'Dot's bigger den mine, yah?' he says in his Swede accent and Emil says, 'Yah. So what?' and Eino goes, 'Too dem big, Emil,' and reaches down and cuts the line.

"By this time they're all laughing like hyenas. I never heard a bunch of grown men laugh so much. They threw away a forty pound fish right in front of our eyes. What could we do but laugh, too? We all rode back together and got drunk and ate northern pike fillets. Coated 'em with pancake mix and fried 'em up. Even I got enough to eat that time."

Jon was going to have to drink and eat for about three days to make up for all the talking he had just done. He ordered chicken while the rest of us turned our attention to the drinking contest. Santoni was ahead by two drinks.

"I just don't have it," lamented the old man. "They don't go down like they used to."

150

"You just need to get back in shape," Rich said. "Give yourself a couple weeks to get in training."

"Maybe you ought to be careful now," Matt countered. "It might not be a good idea to drink so much with you being sick."

The old man stared at him without replying.

I went to play pool with Jon's kids. They were fair shots but couldn't concentrate very long, so I managed to win two games. Matt came over after a while to see if here were finally some pool players he could beat.

The tavern got crowded as the night wore on, but the noise level stayed low. It was quite gloomy, actually, and I wondered why anybody from the town would choose to go there. It was a good setting for Aldridge's mood, however, which grew more and more foul as he realized he couldn't drink with the ease to which he was accustomed.

His stay in the hospital had brought him down to Santoni's level. He was managing to keep up with the tally, more or less, but it was an expensive effort to get each drink down. He passed through a couple of bad stages of nausea and awful skin color, just as Santoni had in most of the whiskey bouts previously, and the rest of us sat in silence while he struggled, looking at the clock, hoping that the bar would close so that we wouldn't have to endure his labored drinking and the combined unpleasantness of his mood and the atmosphere of the bar.

He persevered until closing time, however, and recovered some of his former dignity by finally accepting the slower pace. He had made the decision to go ahead with the contest and now, though the difficulties were proving extreme, his seriousness didn't waiver. He simply put the needs of his body aside and continued drinking. His strength in adversity was remarkable.

For the first time that strength had no noticeable negative effect on Santoni. Though his enthusiasm for the contest had diminished lately due to concern for the old man's health and his consistent second place status, he had welcomed the chance to go easy on a whiskey night and had put the drinks away smoothly until one o'clock. When he saw that the old man wasn't going to suddenly overtake him, he began to drink with more and more confidence. The ending was the same tortured overcoming of nausea that it always was, however. With sweat pouring down his pale, chubby face, he looked grateful to have squeaked out a win.

The total, though not on par with previous sessions, was still substantial. Aldridge finished at nineteen drinks to Santoni's twenty-two. The old man had lost this, the first session since his stay in the hospital, but remained in the overall lead by four drinks. At that point we all figured that, with his extraordinary determination and Santoni's recent lack of competitive spirit, he would soon get his form back and force his opponent to retire after another five of six sessions.

"Any damn fool can condemn what he doesn't understand," Aldridge said to Big Jon on his way out. Jon nodded as if he, at least, did understand.

Twenty

Santoni was highly encouraged by his victory in Clare. He
brought the next session close to home by selecting a quaint tavern
called the Blue Gingham Inn near Cadillac. The place was a quiet,
family style hamburger shop during the day and he chose it partly
to appease several members of the group who were questioning
the good sense in continuing the contest when the old man was
suffering so much. It was supposed to be a comfortable place so
he could relax while competing.

Aldridge made it clear that all this concern for his condition
was wasted. During a round of phone calls between Ann Arbor,
Brighton, and Traverse City, he insisted to one and all that he was
going to go ahead with the contest even if he had to drive to
Santoni's house and compete at the dining room table in front of
his wife and kids. Rich called me a few days before the session to
confirm the old man's determination.

"He says he wants to go ahead," he told me. "I don't see what we can do to stop him."

I had let myself be convinced that Aldridge was engaged in a noble fight to defend the old ways despite his difficulties, and that he was on the side of honor and glory.

"I don't see why we should try to stop him," I said. "It's his life. He can spend it any way he chooses. This is something he cares about."

It sounded good to say it, at least.

"By the way," Rich said, "what did you do to Ken? Bob says he refused to come to this session. He doesn't want to be in the same building with you."

"That's odd," I said. "Maybe he doesn't like losing at eight-ball all the time."

Santoni still managed to get the support of his mistress and her water skiing brother, along with two of his friends who weren't associated with Ken. They had all ordered the delicious hamburgers offered by the Inn when I showed up with J.P.. He usually didn't attend the out of town sessions, but his shop was closed for renovations and he had decided to come to see the action.

On the drive up, we had discussed the outlook of the contest, the seriousness of the old man's health problems, and his determination to continue. J.P. felt that Aldridge was in a very vulnerable position and that his conviction was a means of covering up his insecurity. Having a natural ability suddenly taken away can be very hard to deal with, he said, speaking from the experience of losing an eye. You eventually adjust, but it takes time and your personality usually undergoes some changes. He felt that the next couple of sessions would determine the outcome of the contest.

He went on to say that, having talked to Mrs. Aldridge, he knew of the old man's fondness for my articles. He suggested that they were the critical factor in keeping the old man going.

"Russ is a sensible guy. If he's having that much trouble drinking there's no reason he wouldn't just throw the whole thing over. What does he care about Santoni and a bunch of green kids? No, the thing of it is, he sees a chance to do something here. He sees a chance to make a kind of history."

This terrified me. I immediately suggested dropping the whole idea. Faced with bald reality, I wanted nothing more than to see him quit drinking right away. Responsibility for the old man's life was just the kind of thing I was trying to avoid in my own.

Maybe, I pointed out, I can get him to give it up by throwing out the stories.

"Only a kid would say such a stupid thing," J.P. pointed out generously. We were approaching the inn and he slowed the car.

"It's not up to you anymore, is it? If you quit now, then what's he got to live for? Sure, there's his wife and a few more fishing trips, but if a man lives long enough he gets so he can't clearly see that kind of thing. There's this one thing that has gotten to seem like his mission now. Take it away and there's nothing for him but to die."

He rolled to a stop between two other cars and shut off the engine.

"But he's killing himself anyway with this drinking," I said. Ticking sounds came from the engine compartment as the moving parts settled to a stop. It was starkly quiet after being in a moving car for over two hours.

"You don't know that," he lectured, "and anyway, if he is, at least that's the way he wants to go out. You can't be the one to take that away from a man."

On the telephone a few days before I had said virtually the same thing to Rich, but now that I was faced with the truth I realized I had just been blowing a lot of hot air.

157

Santoni and his friends greeted us when we came in and invited us to sit with them. His mistress greeted me enthusiastically, perhaps forgetting that I was wasting my life, and asked me how my stories were coming along. She had heard about the articles, too.

"What stories?" I asked.

Rich and Matt were due to show up any minute, as was the old man. Some friend of his was making the drive from Traverse City to Royal Oak and had agreed to drop him on the way. I ordered a Sprite to try to calm my stomach, which was souring due to the quick education in responsibility I had received on the drive up.

Our group sat at two tables and chatted amiably for an hour before the old man showed up. His friend turned out to be the man he had shot eight-ball with at the Zukey Lake Tavern a few months before. They both came in along with the friend's daughter, who I thought was stunning.

"I didn't know you guys were such good friends," I said to the man, who introduced himself as Pete Pressly. His daughter's first name was Amanda. "Mr. Aldridge told me you were just acquaintances."

"That's basically correct," he said, "but we ran into each other out on the Rapid River the other day. We began talking, and when I found out that Russell was coming down this way, I offered him a ride. He said one of you others could take him home this evening."

Amanda looked to be in her mid twenties and was staring at me as if I were either a Martian or some kind of celebrity. When I went up to the counter with the old man to order drinks for the group, I leaned close to him and asked, "What's with the girl?"

He looked at me and peered over his shoulder at her.

"Beat's me," he said.

After half an hour of conversation, the bar telephone rang and the waitress called Santoni to the counter. He spoke on the phone for a few minutes then came back to the table grinning.

"Rich and Matt hit a deer," he said. "Anybody want to go pick 'em up?"

The best combination of drivers was discussed at length. Santoni and Aldridge considered going, one being the brother of the indisposed car's driver and the other depending on the missing member for his transport home, but both had had at least two beers by this time and it was decided that they should stay and start the match. Santoni's mistress said "I'm not going," and that possibility was therefore completely foreclosed. Her brother's driver's license was suspended – as it was most of the time – because he apparently drove a car and a boat by following the same instruction manual. The two salesmen were about to be recruited when Santoni said, "Why don't you two go?"

He was referring to me and Mr. Pressly's daughter. There was a note of complicity in his voice along with a smile that suggested he was doing me a favor by putting her in the car with me.

"Neither of you has had anything to drink yet, have you?"

Her father welcomed the chance for a respite from traveling and offered his car. I knew the roads, so I was handed the keys. Amanda looked a little nervous about being stuck in the car with me, but was apparently too shy to try to run away. Those who remained were to start the contest right away. We confirmed Rich and Matt's location in Mt. Pleasant and went out to the parking lot.

"You want to drive?" I asked.

"Will you, please?" she asked. "I've actually been driving all morning."

Their car was a big old Impala in perfect condition. We sat far apart on the front bench seat. I adjusted the mirrors, checked the gauges, and fastened my seatbelt before starting the engine and setting out for Mt. Pleasant.

The tree lined road moved past, slowly at first, then faster, accompanied by the hum of the motor and the rush of the tires on the asphalt. We didn't talk for some time. She began to fiddle with the radio. After dialing through about a dozen stations, she selected country music.

I began to think about the problem of the old man and my articles. What J.P. had said seemed to make sense, and it left me with a bad feeling. I did not want to contribute to the demise of an old man, especially one for whom I had so much respect, but it was going to be very difficult to write any more with that weight hanging over me. On the other hand, it occurred to me that I hadn't shown him everything I had written. If I truly couldn't write any more, then I could just drag out the old ones and show them to him when he asked. Maybe I was making too much of the whole thing. It wasn't as if I was forcing him to continue, I thought, but that idea didn't much help to lift the weight I felt.

Amanda pointed out a family of raccoons scuttling along the side of the road. I was about to ask where she and her father lived, but just as I opened my mouth, she began to speak.

"I hear you're going to be a famous writer," she said with an ironic smile.

At that moment I sincerely wished I had never written even one word.

"So you've heard about those articles, too," I said. "Everybody's making way too much of them. I can't even get 'em published."

"Well, Mr. Aldridge thinks they're great. And I never met a writer before."

She was way too nice to treat with the disdain I usually reserved for such situations, but I tried to talk her out of this untenable position. I explained that writing was just something people do, like any other activity, and that at first they're usually full of imagination but poor at the craft. They get better by practicing, just like any other activity. I was probably not much good at it myself.

She protested that it seemed impossible to her. She said that she enjoyed reading fiction and that she became totally absorbed in books written by her favorite writers. She couldn't imagine being able to create a totally imaginary world, she said. Neither could I, I said.

It turned out that she had just gotten her degree in Natural Resources and was working with the state's salmon planting program. She dismissed it as dumb manual labor at first, but when

162

I asked her a few questions it was easy to see that transplanting and raising salmon was fascinating work and that she cared a lot about it. She actually blushed when I told her Aldridge's story about the failed lake trout experiment.

She said she loved fishing, camping, and hiking. Without realizing how out of character it was for me, I suggested that we get together sometime to go fishing in lower Michigan. She seemed happy about the idea and we exchanged telephone numbers.

Rich's car had been towed to a body shop for repairs and the mechanic had promised to have the engine operational by the next evening. Rich and Matt were waiting outside the shop, armed with Polaroid snapshots of a huge set of antlers stuck through the windshield. They looked at me oddly while we stowed their bags in the trunk, clearly wondering who my new friend was, and we all got in the car. Rich jumped in the front passenger seat and Amanda got in the back with Matt without protest. I introduced everybody.

It seemed that while the police were taking information from Rich and Matt, an opportunistic motorist had stopped and swiped the deer carcass.

"I sort of wanted it," Rich said, "but it would have been a hassle to take it to the DNR to get it tagged. We just let him take off with it."

He showed the photos and told the whole story again after we arrived back at the Blue Gingham. Mr. Pressly said that he wanted to get to Royal Oak before nightfall and that they better get going, so I again promised to call Amanda about fishing and we bid them goodbye. After they went out the door the old man looked at me with his characteristic half smile.

"Have a nice drive?" he asked.

"Very nice," I said. He just nodded.

We rearranged the separate tables into one long conference table and they filled us in on the progress so far. To press his advantage, Santoni had chosen white Russians, a drink so sweet that my own limit would have been three or four, if even that many. Santoni was ahead nine drinks to six, so it looked like a typical sweet drink session so far.

"How's the drinking?" I asked the old man, who shrugged his shoulders.

"Let's get back to it," he said.

He and J.P. were playing cribbage while they drank and Santoni was playing backgammon with his girlfriend.

"WHAM!" Rich said to the water skier, on the subject of the deer. "I couldn't believe that sucker jumped right into the windshield.

"I wish I could've seen it," said the water skier.

"I can't remember a thing," Matt said. He had been asleep until just after the collision. J.P. offered to do the body work on the car when Rich brought it back to Ann Arbor.

The atmosphere in these recent sessions was much less intense than in the earlier ones. Aldridge and Santoni chatted jovially to one another while drinking. The pace was slower. Santoni had learned something about over extending himself. His early fast drinking was slightly curtailed and he drank steadily at the more reasonable pace throughout the evening. I couldn't imagine how anybody could go on drinking these horrible drinks into the fifteen and twenty drink range, but he and even the old man kept slurping one down every twenty minutes or so.

There was no pool table, and rest of us tried to keep ourselves busy with cribbage, backgammon, and Rich's variations on the theme of the deer-car collision. By midnight he had told the story five or six different ways and was becoming an expert on how to kill wild animals with automobiles.

"Nothing to it," he said. "You just make sure to get 'em broadside. Try to clip the legs as you go in, and POW! A hundred pounds of meat. I figure they suffer less than they do when they're shot. BANG! The lights go out."

"Well," said the old man. Everybody turned to look at him. He had been quiet for some time.

"A dog isn't a deer," he said, "and I don't know how much more sense you can make than that, but I've seen a couple things in the field of animal termination by vehicle that might go against your theory."

Rich was a little impatient at losing the spotlight but, with an opening like that, everybody wanted to hear the old man's story.

"This is another Wisconsin story. Sorry to keep leaving our great home state, but I was up there one time fishing with my wife's uncle and his cousin and we were driving over to put in at the public marina near the Burgess'.

Now that he was talking he needed some more sensible lubrication for his throat, so he ordered a bottle of Heineken.

"My wife's uncle's cousin has a big family – six kids – and he drives a station wagon. A big Chevy, if I recall. We had the boat hitched to the back of that and we were headed down Highway Two at a pretty good clip. This was right at the beginning of the

166

fifty-five mile an hour speed limit, so we must have been doing around sixty.

"That boat was a small cabin cruiser. We've fished six in it, so it's no small dingy. Between that and the station wagon I figure we weighed three or four tons."

The beer came and he enjoyed the first half directly from the bottle. He set it down, smiled, and belched quietly. Santoni's mistress got up to go to the ladies room. We all watched her until she was out of sight around the corner.

"It was raining, too," continued the old man, "lightly. Just as we pass Mikey Harrell's place, these two giant black shapes come racing across the grass toward the road. One of 'em turned off just before the road, but the bigger one kept going. Jumped right out in front of us.

"There wasn't even time to think about the brakes until after we hit him. It was a big black lab. And with all that weight on the back we didn't come to a full stop for a quarter mile. We had to leave the car and the boat and walk back because there was too much traffic to back it up. He had slid clear to the other side of the highway. Out cold. Dead, we figured. He was a big son of a bitch. Looked to be over one hundred fifty pounds.

"Naturally we figured it was one of Mikey's dogs, because he's got two or three labs besides his setters. We went up to his place and he came out, but all his dogs were there. Sure enough, the one that had turned off just before running into the road was one of his."

He took another long draught of beer and sat breathing for a moment. Santoni ordered another round of drinks for the contest, and he and Matt started another game of backgammon. Rich was staring intently at the scoring book.

"We stood around with Mikey for a while, discussing what to do about the dog. No, he didn't know anybody around there who had a lab or a Newfie that size. Of course he couldn't stop other dogs from coming around with his bitches howling all the time. He could ask around, though.

"Just as we were going to go over and pick that fellow up and take him to the pound, he lifted his head up. We're all staring at him, you know, since we thought for sure he was dead. In a minute he stands up, pretty as you please, and shakes off like he just got out of the water. He looked over at us for a second, then just started off down the roadside. Didn't even limp. Never saw him again."

A few moments passed while we visualized the incredible dog strolling down the highway. Then one of the salesmen started in with a story about his own experience in car crashes. Rich began to elaborate on the differences between predators and deer and the role of their body composition in collisions with cars. Aldridge turned his attention back to drinking. Matt offered to play Santoni's lady friend in cribbage.

The extent of the old man's loss of ability was becoming starkly clear at this point. He was unable to accelerate the pace of his drinking at all, and when Santoni initiated a strategic blitz of three drinks, the old man could do nothing but watch his opponent get further ahead. Though in the past he might have taken exactly the same action with the hope that Santoni would lose control later on, this time the atmosphere of his inaction was one of helplessness.

Even as he obviously lost momentum, however, he was able to maintain his extraordinary poise. He saved face by devoting his attention to the board games and to listening to the personal history of Santoni's mistress. Though he drank more slowly than before, he did so with the same calmness and lack of expression he had always had.

Santoni, for his part, had come a long way. Beside regulating the pace of his drinking much better than he had in the past, he had stopped playing silly games to try to unbalance the old man. He had been gaining confidence in his ability to drink steadily and long during the first ten sessions, even while consistently losing, and the recent win proved to him that he could outdrink the old man even in bourbon territory. He was polite about Aldridge's new weakness in that he didn't refer to it or try to set an excruciating pace, but at the same time he wasn't shy about showing his strength. With his ability improving every session, this one would probably have been intensely competitive if the old man had been well.

As it was, Santoni pulled further and further ahead. In the last hour, while the old man continued to finish his single drink every twenty minutes, Santoni swallowed six of the horrible drinks. He seemed to be having no trouble with nausea, even with all the sugar, and ended up being quite calm, though his hair was matted to his head with sweat, as usual. He nodded seriously at the end of the evening when Rich announced the results.

The old man shook his head and smiled ruefully. He had been able to make a total of twenty-one drinks, which was respectable on any sweet drink night and showed that he was beginning to get at least some of his strength back. But Santoni was at full strength and had reached twenty-seven. For the first time since the contest began, Santoni had the overall lead and there was no sign that he intended to give it up.

Twenty-One

Word went around that the old man was depressed. We heard that his wife had joined the many voices calling for him to retire from the contest and that he was having trouble dealing with the combined effects of over drinking and the drugs he was taking to combat his illness. A contest session had been scheduled for one week after the session at the Blue Gingham but, the night before it was to start, Rich called everybody to explain that it had been postponed "for a week or two." When I tried to call the Aldridge place near Traverse City, there was no answer.

I got hold of J.P., who said that Santoni was at home in Brighton, but other than that he didn't have much more information than anybody else. We made plans for me to go out to his place in Chelsea over the weekend to help him repair his boat. The fiberglass on one side had been damaged by a deadhead in Little Portage Lake and I had offered to help if he'd let me borrow the boat a few times. We agreed to meet on Sunday.

I called Santoni later, mostly because I had been all ready to take the bus up to Traverse City the next day and couldn't sit still without finding out more about Aldridge. His wife answered the phone in a quiet voice and asked me to wait.

"What do you hear about the old man?" I asked when he picked up the phone.

"Same as you, I guess," he said. He sounded much more subdued than he did at the drinking sessions. "I think he's camping with his wife this weekend, trying to get his strength back. She's trying to talk him into quitting."

We talked about her influence and decided that it probably wouldn't be much if his heart was set on continuing. Aldridge was old fashioned in many ways and, we figured, as much as he loved his wife and let her run things at home, he didn't think women had an equal say in important matters. Also, Santoni reminded me, she had been against the contest from the beginning, a fact I guess I hadn't been fully aware of until then. She had regarded the contest, he said a bit sullenly, as being a silly waste of time for an old man like her husband.

"What do you think?" I asked him. He hesitated before answering.

"He's done a hell of a job," he said. "I never expected him to be so tough."

"Yeah. By now you must have thought about pulling out for his sake. People must be asking you about it, anyway."

"Right. People have asked me about it."

"And?"

"And now you're asking me?"

"I'm just asking," I said.

"All I can say is that nobody was asking him to quit for my benefit when he was kicking my ass all over the place before he got sick. And in case people haven't noticed, he still wants to keep going. He's a tough old bird. Look at those drink totals lately. You got to respect him for that, and I'm not going to be the one who pulls the rug out from under him. I'm going to try to win."

"But how long is it going to go on?"

"Until one of us quits," He said. "You know that."

Twenty-Two

Near the end of August the old man had to be in Ann Arbor for some medical tests, so he decided to stay in town for the next session. On August thirtieth we met at the Old Town for lunch, and over turkey sandwiches we started talking about making a trip to Grand Marais for the Menominee run in late October.

"Your girlfriend might like to come along for that one," he said before sipping from a glass of Heineken.

"Girlfriend?" I asked.

He swallowed his beer and wiped his mouth with a napkin. We were sitting at a table in the front part of the tavern so we could look out the window and watch people passing on the sidewalk. He gazed out while he spoke.

"You might as well bring her," he said. "I can't imagine a better way to get things off on the right foot."

"You mean all the healthy exposure to our gang of drinkers and philanderers?" I asked.

"I mean fishing, wise-ass," he said, grinning his old man's grin. His S's were sounding a little odd and he pushed against his teeth with his thumb.

"Damn fool things," he said. "Take care of your teeth. The replacements they've got worked out aren't worth a tinker's damn."

He heaved a sigh and stared into his beer. He had lost some weight in his face and it made him look a little healthier, but his physical strength and positive mood came and went at short intervals.

"Getting old is the shits," he said suddenly, fixing me with his gaze. "Who'd have thought that an upstart punk like Santoni would beat me in a drinking contest? He's so green I can't even believe they let him into the bar.

"You know, you go along with a skill you've trained for, say, fifty years or so, then one day you wake up and you realize that Mother Time has been stealing it from you, bit by bit, all along. Some pup takes a swing at you and you've got to duck it and walk away."

I was surprised to hear him talking this way and told him so.

"If you want to win this thing, you still can," I said. "Santoni hasn't beat you yet."

He peered at me with the disdain he usually reserved for "damn fools."

"Barring miracles," he said, "he has won."

We finished our lunches and resumed making plans for the trip north in October, lamenting the difficulty in finding an adequate supply of waxworms. Other baits worked, but not as well, and since ice fishing season didn't start until December the bait shops didn't usually stock many waxworms until then. He was going to try to order some in advance from Neff's.

I paid the tab and we went out, me holding the door and waiting for him to catch up. He stepped slowly down the four stairs to the sidewalk, stopping on one step to stare into the distance as though something of significance were taking place on the horizon. He breathed audibly through his nose.

We walked past three doorways to the Liberty Inn. The old man crossed the threshold with a grouchy shrug. Nobody liked the place any better than they had in the spring, but Santoni hated the atmosphere as much as anybody, and that's what convinced Aldridge to choose it. He was going for broke on what he saw as his last chance to pull out a come-from-behind win.

The lunchtime crowd had left and the bar was nearly empty. Nobody from our group had arrived yet. We took the last table in the back near the pool table, sitting with our backs to the wall and facing the bar.

"Drink a beer?" the old man asked me. There was an unusual note of confidentiality in his voice. I nodded seriously.

"Yeah," I said, "something in a bottle."

"Two Heinekens, Pam," he said to the waitress, "and a bag of chips for this young man."

We sat in silence for a few minutes after our beers arrived, admiring the ugly blue paint on the walls and the landscape mural, lighted from behind, that remained in the space behind the bar from the days when this was a place the old timers actually enjoyed visiting. The waitress and the bartender talked quietly near the beer taps, and there was some vile daytime show on the TV set at the far end of the bar.

"How are the articles coming?" he finally asked. I was surprised at how difficult it was for him to ask the question.

"Okay," I shrugged. "It's been a little hard to write since you got sick."

177

He reached over and picked up my bag of chips, still unopened. He fumbled with the fold of wrapper at the top before managing to pull it open. He took a few chips out and set it back on the table in front of me.

"Don't let it worry you," he said. "That's for the damn fool doctors and me. You have more important things to concern yourself with."

Then, after a pause, he asked, "any more finished?"

"A few," I said, congratulating myself for holding some back when I showed them to him the first time. "You want to see 'em?"

He nodded, then looked directly at me. "That's right."

"Let me get them into some kind of shape. Couple days, maybe. Then I'll bring some over."

He nodded again. The music had stopped. I could see he was about to share another difficult thought.

"The reason I ask is ..."

"Yeah?" my gut tightened.

"... I'm thinking of giving it up, finally. Hate to do it, but ..."

Actually hearing him say it hit me hard. I wasn't sure whether it was happiness that he was getting out, or regret. Even though I was deeply worried about his health, I had gotten used to my outward heroics in favor of his continuing and it was tough to make the sudden transition.

"Why now?" I asked, my voice sounding a little high and odd. Before he could speak, I added, "I mean, I think I know why, but what made you finally decide to quit now. I mean, really decide?"

"The truth?" he said, staring at the far wall now instead of at me. "Hell, I guess I haven't decided, not one hundred percent. It still depends on today, maybe the next session."

He took a long gulp of beer from his glass.

"But there are two major factors, now that you ask," he said after clearing his throat. "One is that it's damn foolishness to compete when you don't stand a fool's chance in hell of winning. The other is my wife. She's ready to blow her stack. You know how women are. Or maybe you don't, not yet, but a man has certain responsibilities once he's married and I have to give her opinion the weight it deserves."

Which demolished all the highly logical arguments Santoni and I had shared on the phone a couple of weeks before. I nodded again.

"Sounds reasonable enough. Everybody else wants you to give it up, that's for sure."

He looked directly at me again. There was just the faintest trace of relief on his face.

"So," he said, "you don't mind my dropping out? You think you can finish up your articles anyway?"

"Oh, hell," I said, "I can't believe you're asking me. I can't believe you've stuck it out this long. I know I couldn't have done it. I'm ..."

I'm glad you're going to give it up, is what I had begun to say, but suddenly I felt my belly contract with grief and my eyes fill up with tears. I hardly knew why I was so upset but, trying to make it look like a coughing fit, I slid my chair back, stood up and walked into the men's room. There I locked myself into the stall and sobbed like a baby. I had to lean against the wall for support, my hand over my mouth to keep the sounds from escaping.

It had been at least twenty years since I cried like that and I wasn't even sure why I was doing it. Reflecting back on that day, I suppose now that it was partly out of relief, since it meant that I wouldn't have to bear the great sense of responsibility I felt for his life, however much that feeling was misplaced. It was also because he had placed so much confidence in my opinion, almost asking

180

my permission to quit, which made me feel for a moment like an equal to him, and because the contest, which had become such a big part of my life, was going to end. But at the time I couldn't parse my emotions with such clarity. It was nearly ten minutes before I could bring myself to go back out to the table.

When I did go out Santoni, Rich, Matt and J.P. had all arrived. They had rearranged the chairs around the table and had just sat down. My half-empty bottle of Heineken sat before the only empty chair. The waitress came over to take drink orders.

"Star Treks and chasers," said the old man. "Of course."

Santoni laughed, said, "dammit," and leaned back in his chair. Everybody was going to drink along with the contestants for the first five drinks to help them get started. When the shots came, I swallowed mine at once. I needed something to dull the confusion I felt at my sudden outburst of emotion. The sharp taste of the bourbon stung my throat, but its warm glow helped to steady my hands.

The old man didn't comment on what had happened to me, but he was in contest mode, which meant that the expression of emotions was temporarily suspended. Every action was calculated to affect his opponent. He and Santoni faced one another and, though the atmosphere was still relatively relaxed, it was easy to see that he was going to compete for all he was worth.

The first few rounds followed the model for drinking that had been the hallmark of the contest in the early sessions. Santoni, in an effort to avoid the taste of the drinks, slammed down six in such a hurry that we thought he would get sick before dinnertime. He stated, however, that the chasers were helping smooth the way for the bourbon. The old man proceeded at his noble and measured pace through four drinks, until the others decided to get something to eat.

"Yuppie food," he stated with disgust, looking over Matt's shoulder at the menu. He asked the waitress for another bag of chips. The others ordered various ordinary sandwiches with overblown names and inflated prices.

"How'd your car come out?" he asked Rich.

"Oh man," Rich said, "it looks great. By the time J.P. got through with it, it looked better than it did before the damned deer. There was this squeak in the front end for the last five thousand miles and now that's gone. Replaced all the carpet inside, too."

J.P. smiled humbly. "I had some of that carpet lying around the shop from another project. The color just happened to match."

The drink count was eight to five when the food arrived and, true to form, the old man caught up while Santoni was eating. He seemed unaffected by the drinks so far and it looked like it was going to be a good match. After the meal, someone pulled out a backgammon board. J.P. and the old man went to the pool table and started a game of eight-ball. People were drifting in to fill the bar and the two men wanted to get a start on the pool table before it became impossible to get a turn.

"Last pocket?" J.P. asked.

"Yup," said the old man.

The games went smoothly for about an hour without much conversation. An acquaintance of Santoni's had joined the party and was advising Matt on how to best utilize each roll of the dice.

"Take the six point," he was saying. "Your best odds are on the six point and then his chances of getting out of your home board decrease by at least half."

He was standing and couldn't see Matt's sour expression.

Two young guys who had been at the early sessions came in and sat at the table next to ours. After Matt had beaten Rich by ignoring all the advice offered by Santoni's friend, he moved over to the other table and let the advisor play against the old man.

Aldridge was going to finish up the eight-ball game while taking on the advisor.

Hamming it up in his role as the old master, Aldridge pushed up his sleeves and looked seriously at the board. He winked at one of the young men. Matt, in his new seat at the next table, was sitting near me.

"How'd things work out with that girl?" he asked me.

"Girl?" I said. I had just received my fifth Jim Beam, straight up with a small beer chaser.

"That girl you were with when you drove us back to the Blue Gingham. She wasn't bad looking."

"Hmmm," I said.

"Don't let him fool you, Matt," Santoni said. "He's been fishing with her three or four times since then. Her old man actually called me once, wondering where they were."

I stalled innocently, staring into space.

"Yup," J.P. started. "It's got so I can't hardly use my own boat. He's borrowing it every three days. Only good to come out of it is that, with all the miles he's putting on my pickup I'll be able to sell it for new when the odometer turns over."

"No shit?" Matt asked.

When this line of talk died down I admitted that we had gone to Four Mile Lake with J.P.'s boat and caught a few fish.

"Man," he said to me, "you are one sneaky dude. I didn't think you had even noticed her."

"You after that white bass again?" asked the old man. He turned to Santoni's friend and, pointing me out, said, "That kid got a twenty-two pound white bass over in Appleton Lake and you can't even get him to talk about it."

"Twenty-two pounds?" said the man. "That's incredible. It must be some kind of world record. Did you take it to the DNR?"

"He let it go," J.P. said. "Hell, he gets fish like that all the time. I saw him release it. Then he came aboard our boat and drank half our beer."

"Catching fish does make a guy thirsty," I admitted.

"Don't let him pull your leg," the old man joined in after sinking the eight ball. "He got five Chinook over thirty pounds last fall alone. He holds the unofficial state record for brook trout at eight and a half pounds."

I was beginning to be pretty impressed, myself.

"Jesus," the man continued as Aldridge took his winning move in the backgammon game, "I gotta go fishing with you sometime."

"If you can get him away from that girl long enough," somebody said.

Finally, they moved on to other subjects. Aldridge complained that it was still far too difficult to get the drinks down, though at that point he and Santoni were even at fourteen. There was a demeanor about each man suggesting the rest of the evening was going to be intense.

Santoni was drinking with an ease that he had never shown in the early sessions. He said he had learned that the individual drinks themselves were not that important. Instead, he fixed his mind on the goal, which was the total number of drinks at the end of the night. This longer outlook gave him a confidence, or at least a lack of concern, that mirrored Aldridge's poise in the early bouts. And that was in spite of the fact that they were drinking bourbon.

His metamorphosis made me wonder if the old man, too, had had a wider range of tastes when he was younger. If someone as formerly undisciplined as Santoni could learn to drink Jim Beam with such commitment, then might not Aldridge have been very different as a younger man? Had he learned to drink seriously by being exposed to an older, wiser influence? I would have to ask him about it sometime.

Aldridge himself was drinking at speed, but he was concentrating on getting each drink down. Reflecting on past sessions, I realized that the loser often got caught in this trap or was forced into it by physical limitations. Drunkenness alone had long since ceased to be a major factor for either man since they had learned to regulate it by controlling the speed of their drinking. Instead, it was nausea that had taken on a vital role in the outcome of each match. Whereas in the past an upset stomach had not been a consideration for the old man until he drank into the mid-twenty drink range, he now hit a barrier of disgust in the middle to late teens. It was painful to watch him struggle with his diminished ability though, as usual, his effort was almost entirely hidden by his calm and dignified manner. I had to watch carefully to see the discomfort that each drink was costing him. Seeing how awful they must have been, I began to understand one factor in his decision to quit.

His miracle, unfortunately, never came. He pushed himself nearly to blind drunkenness near the end, cursing his doctors and the fates a little with each drink, but Santoni moved steadily ahead after they reached the twenty-drink mark. It was like watching a boxer finishing off a weaker opponent. The younger man had his strength and was delivering very sound, deliberate blows to his foe, who could at first block and counter, but who later could only evade a few of the attacks and, finally, though he could still show his heart by refusing to fall down, could only absorb the punches and wait for the rounds to expire. It was humiliating, but nobody could do anything to stop it.

Santoni's new friend was unaware of everything that had gone into the combat up until that time and loudly praised him for his conquest. I had resolved to give up salesman bashing, viewing the whole business as unsatisfying and leading to fewer available drinking establishments, but I almost went back on my vow before Santoni, having matured in a number of ways, hushed his friend.

The rules we set required that the contest end on an even number of matches. Santoni had a session left to select, or otherwise I think Aldridge might have quit right then. He was disgusted with himself for still being involved in the contest and even more disgusted with himself for losing with a total of only twenty-six drinks to Santoni's very respectable thirty-one. I had to help him to his feet and there was no denying now that he was old and nearly incapacitated.

"God dammit," he said, even his ability to make inscrutable statements gone, finally. "God dammit"

I walked him carefully out to his wife's car, which was parked at a meter across the street. The sidewalks were empty, other than a few pieces of wastepaper skittering across the road in the wind. The first chill of autumn made me shiver in the night air.

Twenty-Three

The contest ended in Traverse City on Tuesday, September seventeenth, which happened to be my birthday. The last drinks to be ordered, chosen by Santoni, were called Long Island Ice Teas, dark brown, sweet drinks served in cola glasses at the Little Bo. The Bo was a tavern frequented by outdoorsmen and working people and it was usually packed on weekends but, on this weeknight, it was only half filled. Somehow it hadn't caught on with the tourists yet, and the few drinkers who were there peered at us suspiciously over their Bud Lights.

The members of our party had all parked their cars in a lot by the Boardman River, where the meters still offered ten hours for a dime, and had walked over. I had ridden the bus up and walked over from the Greyhound station just in time to see the two competitors finishing their first drinks. The atmosphere of the bar was smoky and depressing, all the stains and wear showing in the little pale daylight that was able to shine through the smeared windows. I remember being glad that this would be the last session, because I was getting tired of spending so much time indoors breathing other people's smoke and waking up the next day with a headache and a sour stomach.

In spite of his vow to quit, the old man was not letting up. He forced the pace on the second, third, and fourth drinks, escaping nausea by sipping at a beer between contest gulps. Santoni had dark circles under his eyes from the beginning, having worked fourteen days in a row to earn this weekend off. He didn't look happy about drinking the large drinks quickly, but he knew the end was near and wouldn't give in.

Then, too, his wife had recently discovered his fondness for extracurricular activity with female camp counselors and had all but forbidden him to travel. She had allowed him to go to this session only because she knew the history of the contest and because she knew he would be staying at the old man's house. He would probably find a way to get around the sanctions eventually but, for now, he was humbled and it clearly showed.

Rich, Matt and two new guys had been there since lunchtime shooting pool. Matt was actually winning, having found a way to overcome the tension that had made him choke on critical shots. He had also discovered that eight-ball was better for him than nine-ball. He could build up a lead with his good shooting on the regular balls, then allow himself one or two misses on the eight before his opponent caught up. This meant he was a lot more relaxed during the difficult shots. It was good to see him gaining confidence.

There were no stories this time. The old man played one game of cribbage with me but declined any more games after he won. He sat at the bar and meditated, staring at the rows of bottles and remembering some spectacular fishing trip in a country as yet undiscovered by tourists and waters skiers.

Santoni was becoming more gregarious as the afternoon wore on, talking shop with his new friends. They had met through some distribution deal his company had made and that was their main topic of conversation. I didn't really listen but I did notice that he had been hesitant to meet the old man's gaze. His constant stream of chatter allowed him to slip in orders for drinks and comment on the progress of the contest without being confrontational. I suppose he felt sorry for the old man by that time, or else he simply wasn't sure how to deal with the new imbalance in their abilities. I couldn't blame him for being a little nervous. I wasn't sure what to say about it, either.

I played a couple of close games of eight-ball with Matt, winning one and losing one. I ate a hamburger with lettuce, tomato and extra mayo, and selected a couple tunes on the jukebox. I watched the steady downing of drinks and wondered about the destruction they must have been doing to the old man's insides. The time passed slowly, but it did pass, and quite a few drinks got consumed. The bar gradually filled with cigarette smoke.

Finally, Aldridge, gazing through rheumy eyes at the glass in front of him, made no move to pick up his drink.

"That's seventeen total, right?" asked Rich.

"Seventeen?" echoed Aldridge. He continued to sit without drinking. It was clear that he had finally conceded defeat.

"Without I was sick, we could have been done in July," he said. He asked about the time. Someone told him it was almost nine. Hearing this, he let his gaze swing slowly around to the people nearby.

Early in the contest, they had agreed that for the drinking to be valid the contestants would have to keep their drinks down until the morning following a match. If the old man was really giving up now, then the only thing that might save him was the chance that Santoni would get sick before morning. It didn't seem likely since they had been drinking in the younger man's realm for the past six hours.

There was some quiet speculation about drink numbers and varying effects of alcohol and sugar on the body, including the fact that together they had consumed seven hundred eleven drinks since the beginning of the contest, not including this session. But mostly we were all subdued by the liquor we ourselves had consumed and by the grim fact that the contest was really over.

Aldridge pushed the full glass along the top of the bar to place it in front of his opponent. Santoni sat with his head down, staring at his feet, his face bright red and coated with its customary sheen of sweat. He had finished twenty of the horrible drinks and the old man's unfinished seventeenth drink meant that he had won the night with a margin of four drinks. That placed his overall contest lead at eleven. It might as well have been fifty, given the old man's present state.

When Aldridge stood up to leave, we all stood as well. Two from our entourage bought six packs to drink on the road, and we filed out to our cars. Santoni shuffled along beside Rich to the latter's car. He was walking without bobbing up and down, presumably to avoid upsetting his stomach. His balance seemed questionable. He didn't especially walk like a winner.

When we got back to the house on Cedar Lake, Aldridge retired to his room. The others who had joined us at the house found beds or couches where they could or, in Matt's case, simply fell asleep in the middle of the living room floor.

I washed my face and went down to the TV room. Santoni was watching Johnny Carson and sipping a soda. His glazed, half open eyes were fixed on the screen. He was motionless except for tiny movements of his chest as he breathed. I could feel his sense of loose connection with reality, a kind of loneliness in the satisfaction of winning, perhaps a deep fatigue from driving his body to its limits on so many occasions in recent months.

I went over to the glass door and slid it open. The night air was cool and refreshing and a whippoorwill called in the darkness.

"Hey Bob," I said, "listen to this."

He didn't respond at all. The television bathed his face in pale artificial light. He may have been asleep.

I went back upstairs to the kitchen. Aldridge's wife was washing dishes.

"He's sleeping now," she said of her husband. "Thanks for driving him back."

We talked for a few minutes, then I went to my room. I felt very old myself, having stayed up later and having drunk more in these last six months than good judgment should have allowed. I drank a glass of water and swallowed vitamin pills and aspirin, hoping to prevent the inevitable hangover. I was asleep before midnight.

195

Twenty-Four

The next morning everybody started to prepare for the trip home. This was a group of people with flexible jobs so there was normally no hurry to get back, but fall fishing season was approaching and most of them had to work just enough to get a ten-day break in November.

I had no problem finding an empty seat on the bus, there being only three other people aboard. The weather was clear and cool and I was refreshed by the thought of the cold temperatures of autumn and finally being able to stay away from the bars. As we passed through town, I saw that there were still a few tourists, but most of the people were local types. Hot-rodders gunned up and down Bayview Road, kids walked home from school, women carried shopping bags to their cars, and a few Hispanic fruit pickers walked along the sidewalks, probably in town for the apple season. I remember being pleasantly surprised at the feeling of seeing ordinary people doing ordinary things after having been wrapped up in the drinking contest for so long. A normal working life seemed very attractive all the sudden and I vowed to get a more conventional job when I got back, limit my fishing and drinking to weekends, maybe start getting a little exercise every day.

I thought about Aldridge's summer house on the lake. It must seem very quiet to him now with everybody gone. Just he and his wife, perhaps a grueling hangover following the last duel, his knowledge of the disease already far advanced in his body. It would never be in the newspaper, but drinkers all over Michigan would be commenting on the outcome of the contest. The old man had lived and fished in the state for nearly every one of his sixty-seven years. Wherever we had gone, the old timers greeted him, knew what he drank, and knew what sort of eight-ball he shot. In my own travels around the state, I had run across him a surprising number of times, sitting quietly at a bar, alone or with one or two other drinkers, gazing ahead, sometimes talking with the others about the fishing or the weather.

Thinking back, it's not such a surprise that we would meet. We preferred the same sort of out of the way places, old, quiet, not too far from a good fishing spot. I suppose there weren't more than fifty such taverns in Michigan, if that many, and in twenty years of traveling, early on with family then later alone, I had visited most of them more than once.

Santoni would have gone back to his busy house in Brighton to be with his wife and his two kids. His job demanded long hours when he did work, so his life would soon be full of new demands and he could forget about the contest he had just won. He was only a few years older than me, but had already accumulated all the assorted baggage of the accomplished family man. He could now concentrate on inventing new reasons to drive to northern Michigan.

I had visited his home once, after one of the bouts, when I had a huge batch of perch that I didn't want to eat, or clean, by myself. I had offered him the fish and he accepted, but invited me in for dinner. His kids cleaned all one hundred twenty-five fish. While we ate, and afterwards, he sipped at a Coke, the same one all night. I had to wonder at this delicacy when the night before he and Aldridge had each drunk over thirty whiskeys with small beer chasers.

Santoni's wife was a small, pale woman who didn't talk much. She could cook well, judging by the excellent perch we ate that night, and had a fragility that suggested something less than robust physical health. It concerned me that she was married to a man who drank so much, but she seemed grateful to have him around.

For his part, Bob expended little energy on being polite at home. He got the kids working and his wife cooking and otherwise ignored them while I was there. Nevertheless, his kids adored him.

When we first walked into the house, his wife had asked him how the bout had gone the night before. Instead of answering, he stared vacantly ahead while trying to decide where to set the fish. After a moment, she took them from him. He either smiled or grimaced when she wiped a speck of something off his cheek with the fingers of her free hand.

That was in early May, about a month before Aldridge had gone into the hospital. The night before had been the old man's night to choose.

Part Four

Twenty-Five

Russell Aldridge, the last of the great drinkers in the old style, died at Grand Marais in his rented bedroom at the Sunshine Cabins on the morning of November twenty-ninth, nineteen ninety-one. He was sixty-seven years old but looked at least ten years older, especially to those of us who knew him.

November twenty-eighth had been Thanksgiving Day, even in Grand Marais. The night before there had been an unexpected major storm which dropped fourteen inches of snow, so the fishermen and all the locals had come to the Dunes Saloon, making for an exceptionally large and noisy crowd for a Thursday night. Since the nearest edible turkey dinner was twenty-five miles away at Pine Stump Junction, we stayed put and contented ourselves with good pizza and a football game on the television.

There are always a couple dozen fishermen on the pier at Grand Marais around Thanksgiving for the autumn Menominee run, usually including some variation on the core group of fishermen I had gotten to know over the years. I had either fished or drunk with nearly everyone who was in the bar on the night of the twenty-third, including two doctors from Traverse City, an unemployed fishing buddy from Grand Rapids, three or four salesmen from Ann Arbor, and several union electricians from the East side of the state. I wasn't fishing this year but otherwise everything was about the same as any other year – the eight-ball, the drinking, the revelry.

Aldridge had come to Grand Marais three days before Thanksgiving and, the morning after Thanksgiving Day, he was dead. If the trip hadn't been an ordinary part of his yearly routine it would have seemed that he had gone there specifically to die. The trip had been unexceptional, his last day a day like any other. We shot three games of last pocket in the early afternoon while the Lions lost to Minnesota. He complained of fatigue toward evening and those three were the last games he ever played of his second favorite activity. I was his last opponent, the last person to have a drink with him and, I suppose, I was the last to speak to him other than his wife.

We had gotten to be friends, in our way, during his six months of attempting to uphold the honor of drinking in the old style, for which I had appointed myself the traveling correspondent. The contest, if it can be called exactly that, began in March in Ann Arbor at a drinking establishment called the Eight-Ball Saloon.

The last session took place at the Little Bo in Traverse City. There were fourteen sessions and countless fish stories. My original reporting on the contest consisted of thirty-nine short articles.

This is more writing than it will seem at first because none were written during the month of July when Mr. Aldridge was hospitalized, nor for many months after that. His character was such that he didn't allow even his serious illness to interfere with the contest, though it made his participation far more difficult. Whether the illness would have killed him when it did without the drinking is difficult to say but, when combined with the unlikely quantities of alcohol he consumed, it's a wonder he lived as long as he did. He must surely have known that he was going to die. The last few months of his life were a gradual decline, and finally he was dead.

Twenty-Six

Many years of practice had given the old man exceptional control over himself when drunk. His ordinarily cranky and cynical personality gave way to a quiet, dignified manner, no less imposing for the fact that he sometimes had to depend on others to get around. It seemed more a privilege of age than a handicap for him to require assistance from his younger friends. His eyes were a dark brown color that made them difficult to read and the wrinkled, sunburned skin helped to subdue his expressions. I felt a heavy responsibility to capture that dignity in his obituary, which his wife had asked me to write.

I went to pay my respects to the body while it was still lying in the cabin bedroom. He was covered to the chest with a blanket, but I could see that his wife had dressed him in a light blue dress shirt and beige jacket. I don't know whether he had slept with it on, but it looked like the same shirt he had worn the day before. His hair was combed more neatly than usual, still partly black, though his mustache was almost fully gray.

The color remained in his face. In his repose, I could see that a good deal of his demeanor had been determined by bone structure. Rather than sagging with age, his skin had simply wrinkled in place. Even without any spirit to animate the skin, his face still looked both stern and wise, the features full and well defined. It fit the personality of the man whose life I had to memorialize, and I would not have been very surprised if he had sat up and asked me to play a game of backgammon.

While his wife took care of other arrangements, I went to walk around Grand Marais and think about what I had to write. The snow was blowing, making visibility extremely poor. The wind came off the big lake and blew through me, reminding me of the water's powerful presence and the conversation that the old man and I had shared about the same wind half a year before. There was nothing but the cold, heavy water for hundreds of miles to the north, and above that Canada and who knows what. In the bitter cold his dead face stayed with me, and I couldn't think of a single word to write. There was so little to see in the whiteout of the blowing snow that his image just kept floating in front of me while I trudged through along the unplowed roads. There was Lake Superior and there had been the man. Either you understood such things or you did not, I thought. Everyone who knew him felt a sense of loss. Those who did not, would not.

Out by the pier I watched a couple of cold fishermen huddle over their lines. During the twenty minutes I watched, one of them pulled in just one small fish. It grew too cold to continue standing there so I walked back toward town while they sat hunched over in the profound wind.

Fishing had been Aldridge's favorite activity. So many times it was nothing more than what those two fishermen were doing, just sitting and staring at the motion of the water for hours on end. Perhaps his best quality had been his supreme patience. Or maybe it was resignation.

My thoughts wavered between the simplest possible alternative, the old man's name and age with the time and location of his death, and a fully developed narrative in which I would try to show how his words and actions lent him a power beyond the simple fact of his physical being. I guess all those people referring to me as a writer had begun to have an effect. I ended up sitting in the restaurant in town, warming up with a cup of coffee, a legal pad and a Detroit Free Press on the table. I finished the crossword puzzle in a rush and afterwards felt guilty for enjoying that small pleasure on the day of the old man's death.

It didn't take long to discard the second alternative for his obituary, and the first seemed too short, as though the relatives were embarrassed to make the announcement. Various middle versions occupied three pages of my legal pad, but they were by and large too affected by my writerly aspirations. After all, it wasn't supposed to be my show.

I read the news and whiled away more time. The snow was still blowing around, the skies dark and filled with heavy passing clouds, and the windows of the restaurant were coated with ice. There would not be much more fishing this year.

Around three, Aldridge's wife came in with her sister, who had driven up through the snow from Petoskey to help. They were going to have the body sent to Traverse City and would drive there themselves in the morning. Mrs. Aldridge seemed to be having no great emotional reaction at this point, but the death, after all, had been expected. I asked her a few questions about the old man's earlier life, which she answered dully.

After they left I took my legal pad and crossed the darkening street to the Dunes Saloon. I hoped the atmosphere would give me some inspiration. A dozen people were there, drinking, eating and talking. Nobody was playing pool. Karl came to take my order, which was a beer, soup, and a cheeseburger.

"Too bad about the old man, hey?" he said before going on about his work.

I nodded, and there it was. I was going to accomplish nothing by brooding all day and the old man was, after all, dead. After finishing my beer, I ate my soup and the cheeseburger. I fiddled with a few sentences and ordered a bag of chips and a second beer. I spent another ten minutes getting the wording clean enough to appear in print, then went into the kitchen to borrow Karl's phone. I reached an editor at the Bay City Times and read to him what I had written. The next day it appeared in the paper. Here is how it read:

Thomas Russell Aldridge, age sixty-seven, died in his sleep on the morning of November 29 while vacationing in Grand Marais. Born in Saginaw in 1924, Russ Aldridge served his country in Japan and was given an honorable discharge due to injury in 1948. He took early retirement from the Great Lakes Paper Company in 1971 to enjoy fishing and traveling around the state of Michigan. He is survived by his wife, Vivian Lawrence Aldridge.

About the Author

Nicklaus Suino is a writer, martial arts expert, attorney and business consultant who specializes in the mastery process.

Made in the USA
Charleston, SC
22 March 2013